CYNTHIA EDEN

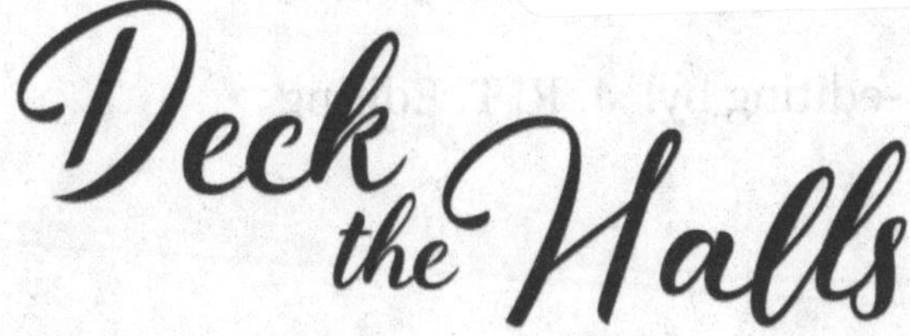

Deck the Halls

CHAPTER ONE

The strains of Elvis's "Blue Christmas" drifted in the air as Christie Tate tried really, *really* hard to disappear inside the women's restroom.

"Did you hear?" The more-than-slightly catty female voice asked from a few feet away.

Christie hunched her shoulders and stared at her heels.

"Charles Crenshaw is already seeing Vicki from accounting. I mean...what's it been? A week? Two? He and Christie were—"

"I think he was seeing Vicki on the side," another female voice chimed in, oozing sympathy.

Fake sympathy.

Christie glanced at the gleaming black door, aware of the heat building in her cheeks. Was this what she'd become? A thirty-year-old woman hiding in a bathroom stall? She knew those voices.

Marsha Chad, a marketing assistant, was the one with the fake sympathy. And the other one—

"I heard Charles thought Christie was just...boring," said Lydia Clyde. "I mean the woman's a genius, but when it comes to men and sex, she's—"

Enough. Christie's spine shot up at the same instant her hand slammed into the bathroom door. The door flew forward, and she caught the sound of two feminine gasps.

Her eyes narrowed as she took in the two women. "Lydia. Marsha." So what if her cheeks were flaming? She wasn't going to hide in the bathroom another second. *Not thirteen anymore. Not the nerdy girl.*

"Christie." Lydia's blue eyes bulged. "I didn't realize you were—"

Christie jerked the faucet on and washed her hands. "For the record..." She lifted her head and met her own gaze in the mirror. *Backbone, girl, backbone.* How many times had she heard her mother say that over the years? *Don't ever let them see you break.* "Sex with me is never boring." She saw their jaws drop. *Good. Great.* She kept her chin up, kept her back straight, and with really fast steps, Christie was able to escape that hellhole.

And trade it for another one.

Christie burst from the women's restroom and walked straight into the full-on madness that was the annual Christmas party for Tate Toys. Bright lights. Elaborate bows. Mechanical toys—trains and soldiers—that marched across the floor. Christmas trees. So many giant, colorful

Christmas trees. Normally, she would have loved the sight, but right then, she just wanted to escape.

She sucked in a sharp breath and tasted pine. Christie glanced to her left and found her ex, Charles, arguing with Vicki under a giant piece of mistletoe. The pretty redhead's hair tumbled down her back as she shook her head at Charles, then she jabbed a finger into his chest. Trouble in paradise?

I think he was seeing Vicki on the side. Lydia's voice whispered through Christie's mind.

Jerk.

A waiter sidled by her. Christie grabbed a flute of champagne and drained it in one gulp. Elvis kept singing.

Can't get much bluer than this, buddy.

She marched forward, putting more distance between her and Charles. *Can't attack.* Because that wouldn't be classy. A lady couldn't go up and jump on her ex's back as she started to pound the crap out of him. A good girl wouldn't do that. She'd been raised to be a *good girl.* Good girls became ladies, right?

But she was damn tired of being good. Damn tired of being gossiped about. Damn tired of it all.

Even tired of Elvis. And she loved the King.

Christie maneuvered through the crowd, stopping only to pick up a few more glasses of champagne. Oh, but that bubbly went down nice and fast. Some folks tried to talk to her, but if they didn't have a tray of champagne flutes near them, she kept going.

Kept going until...

Until she reached the giant black chair that waited in the middle of the room. Santa's chair.

Presents wrapped in red and green paper surrounded the massive chair. Small surprise gifts for all the staff at Tate Toys. Santa would be coming soon. He'd be there to hear all their Christmas wishes. There to make those wishes come true.

Christie's fingers tightened on a champagne flute. Then she caught a glimpse of Santa, and she spilled the rest of her champagne over the front of her red reindeer sweater.

Wow.

Santa was a stud.

Christie swallowed as she got a good look at the jolly old elf. Santa stood just inside the doorway of Tate Toys, a thick, red sack flung over his left shoulder—and what a nice shoulder it was. Actually, Santa had *two* nice shoulders. Nice, wide, broad shoulders that more than filled the red coat he wore.

Her gaze tracked slowly down his body. No shaking like a bowl-full-of-jelly there. Oh, no, that man—*Santa*—was built. Tall, strong. His muscled thighs stretched the red pants and his powerful legs disappeared into a pair of knee-high black boots.

Santa stalked toward her. A fluffy white and fake beard covered his face. A bright red hat hid his hair. All she could see were sparkling green eyes and high, tanned cheekbones.

"Have you been a good girl?" His voice was a dark, deep rumble of sound.

Christie licked her lips. "I—"

"Of course, she has," a voice behind her said with a laugh. Her brother. Jeez, had Daniel caught her ogling Santa? *Can the night get worse?* "You know Christie's always the good one," Daniel added.

At his words, her blood seemed to ice. Right, the good one. That was her. Growing up, she'd been the one closeted away with books while Daniel had been out chasing girls and getting chased by the law.

More laughter floated in the air, and she realized they'd caught the attention of other staff members. Everyone seemed to be watching her. Watching and staring.

Good girl. Good *boring* girl.

That's me.

Her stare flew back to Santa. His head cocked toward her. He seemed to be...waiting. For her?

"Everyone gets a present this year!" Daniel's shout boomed behind her. "We'll start our line, and hey, Christie can be Santa's first victim!"

Victim? Since when did Santa have victims? But everyone was lining up, pushing forward, and they were obviously eager for their gifts. Way eager. Had Daniel put Christmas bonuses in that sack? Knowing him, probably.

Santa set down his bag. Then he rolled his shoulders. Those big, wonderful shoulders, but wait—that roll, that movement was familiar to her. Those green eyes had been familiar, too.

Her heart suddenly beat a little faster.

"Go on, Christie," Daniel urged as he gave her a nudge. "Someone has to get the ball rolling," he whispered the last part in her ear. "You do it, and they'll all do it."

She didn't care what everyone else did.

"Why don't you go and break Santa in, Christie?" Daniel said, raising his voice a bit. "Come on, just go tell the man what you want for Christmas."

Santa had taken his seat on the giant chair/throne. He tilted his head back and stared at her. Then he patted his lap and crooked his finger. At her.

More laughter.

The champagne seemed to burn in her belly. From the corner of her eye, she caught sight of Charles heading toward the end of the growing line. He was minus his new girlfriend.

"Uh, Christie?" Daniel's voice was whisper soft again. "Everyone's waiting."

Let 'em wait. The words were on the tip of her tongue. But a good girl wouldn't say that. A good girl was supposed to do as she was told.

Screw that.

Santa patted his muscular leg again. "Come tell me what you want." His deep voice carried so easily.

Christie shoved her empty flute at Daniel. "Get rid of this, will you?" She sucked in more pine-tasting air and got ready to tell Santa *exactly* what she wanted. Her steps were slow but certain as she approached the Santa Stud and his throne. His eyes were on her, so watchful.

Do it. The whisper came from deep inside. A challenge, a dare. It came from the wilder

Christie, the side she always kept so carefully controlled.

Do it.

What did she have to lose?

She stopped in front of him, and the long edge of her skirt teased his boots. "Um, hi." Right. That sounded confident and sexy. Not.

Santa caught her fingers with his gloved hand and *pulled*. Christie found herself on Santa's lap. A lap that was even harder and stronger up close. Her left hand flew out and pressed against his stomach as she struggled to balance herself.

Definitely not jelly in there. Though she hadn't felt them often in her life, a woman knew rock-hard abs when they pressed against her, even if those abs were hidden by a slightly rough red coat.

"Hello, there." His breath blew against her hair. "No need to be afraid of old Santa."

Obviously, he didn't know her that well. If he did, he would've known that she was afraid of *everything*.

Christie glanced back up at his eyes. Very faint laugh lines graced the edges of his green eyes. No old St. Nick. A Santa in his prime.

A Santa with a toe-curlingly sexy voice.

He released her hand and began to search through his bag of presents. She kept straddling his leg. Not so graceful.

"I'm sure I have something in here for a good girl like you."

She saw red—and not just from his suit. Christie broke as her wild side surged free. She grabbed his hand.

Santa froze. His gaze caught hers once more.

Her heartbeat shook her whole body as she told him, "You don't have what I want in there." She pitched her voice low, not wanting anyone to overhear. "Trust me on this. What I need isn't in that bag."

Those gorgeous eyes narrowed a bit. "What is it that you want for Christmas, pretty lady?"

She leaned in even closer, trying hard to balance on his leg. Santa sucked in a sharp breath, and she was about fifty percent sure she hadn't kneed him in the groin. "I want..."

His head inched toward hers.

The white of his beard tickled her cheek. Christie inched up, heading for his ear. This was a request she needed to whisper.

What am I doing? What?!

Her gaze darted around the room. Daniel was talking to one of the managers, and he seemed totally oblivious to her. From the end of the line, Charles stared at her with a furrow between his pale brows. Marsha and Lydia were in the corner, whispering. Probably talking more smack about her.

Boring...I think he was seeing Vicki while they were together.

Christie's back teeth clenched. *So tired of playing this game. For once, I just want to take what I need.*

"I can keep a secret," Santa told her, his voice quiet. She turned back to him, forgetting the others as he said, "Tell me what you want."

Right then, there was one thing she wanted, and those gleaming eyes seemed to promise it to her. Christie wet her lips, leaned in even closer to St. Nick, and she confessed, "Santa, I want a *really* good time." *Sex with me is never boring.* If only.

He stiffened beneath her, his whole body hardening.

"Know where I can find that?" she asked, her voice husky as she pulled back.

His eyes seemed to burn her. "Oh, I think I—"

"Come on, Christie!" Daniel called out. "Stop hogging Santa! We've got a line here."

She eased off Santa's lap. He grabbed her wrist and held tight.

"I know," Santa finished, that deep voice sending a tremble right through her. "I know exactly where you can find that."

Oh, she just bet he did. Christie tugged her hand free and hurried back as the champagne-induced courage began to desert her.

"Wait, Christie!" Daniel hurried toward her. "You didn't get your present! You can't—"

"Maybe I'll get it later." She brushed by him as her heart raced too fast. *What did I just do?*

"Don't worry. She'll definitely get her present later."

Oh, hell. *His* voice. She'd propositioned the sexy Santa...and the guy had accepted her offer. Offer. Invitation. Wish. Whatever it had been...he sure seemed to be saying...

I'll give you that good time.

***

Jonas Kirk watched Christie Tate's sweet ass as she all but ran away from him. Her words echoed in his ears.

Santa, I want a really good time. Holy shit. Had the woman wanted to give him a heart attack? Or just a serious hard-on?

"Dude...*the presents*," Daniel growled the words.

Jonas realized he was straining to see Christie's ass. Couldn't really help that. The woman had a first-class ass. Put that with her come-and-get-me, blue bedroom eyes and the mouth made for sin, and you had a woman who'd been tempting him for years.

And she'd just asked me for sex.

Screw the presents. Jonas waved his hands toward the bag. "Christmas bonuses are inside...come and get 'em!"

Daniel's eyes—several shades lighter than Christie's—bulged. "What are you doing?"

The crowd swarmed.

Jonas yanked off his beard. "Spreading Christmas cheer." He shoved through the group. Sure, he'd promised his buddy that he'd pop in and play Santa, and Jonas didn't really mind the gig. It was a nice break from his usual routine of catching criminals but—

He knew Christie, and he knew when the woman was about to run. After all, she'd spent most of her life running from him.

Because she knows how much I want her?

He'd always tried so hard to hold the hunger in check when he was around her. Sweet Christie Tate. The girl genius who'd been dropped in his college class even though she was only sixteen. The girl with the slow, innocent smile. The girl who *always* smelled like strawberries. The girl who'd become a woman he craved. A woman who'd been wearing a giant hands-off sign for so long.

A woman he wasn't about to let vanish.

He rounded the corner and caught a glimpse of her hair, long and black, right before the elevator door closed.

Shit.

Jonas shoved open the stairwell door and rushed down the stairs. If he was lucky, he'd catch her in the lobby. A few moments later, his palm shoved into the stairwell's exit door. He ran into the lobby, aware of the guard jumping to his feet with wide eyes.

"It's okay, Jamie." Jonas recognized the guard—a cop who worked after hours at the toy company to get a little extra cash for the holidays. Several of the cops in the area pulled guard duty at the toy shop. "I'm just trying to catch—"

The elevator dinged, a soft peal of sound, and then the doors slid open.

Christie glanced up, and her eyes widened when she saw him. "J-Jonas?"

He lunged through the doors and caught her elbows. He pulled her close. She immediately stiffened. Why was she so tense? Was she regretting her confession now that she saw the man who'd been beneath the beard?

Can't back out. Won't let her.

His lips crushed down on hers. Jonas caught her gasp with his mouth, took in that soft rush of breath, and then his tongue dipped past her lips.

Champagne and strawberries. Figured she'd taste that damn good. A growl built in his throat. *Addictive*. Yeah, he'd always known one taste would probably push him over the edge. Good to know he'd been right.

Her hands rose to his shoulders. Small, delicate hands. *She* was small and delicate. A dancer's body on a woman who always swore she didn't have an ounce of grace.

He expected those hands to push against him. To shove him back. Instead, her fingers curled over him, and Christie pulled him closer. She rose onto her toes, stretching her body against his, and she opened her mouth wider.

Sweet hell.

Her tongue touched his. His entire body went on high freaking alert. They stumbled back a few steps. His hands—then her shoulders—hit the rear wall of the elevator.

The things she could do with her tongue...

Ding.

Jonas wrenched his head up. What was that sound—

Christie's mouth pressed against his throat. Her tongue licked over his skin, and the edge of her teeth lightly bit him.

The damn Santa pants were *too* tight over a certain eager portion of his anatomy. A portion that couldn't wait to be a whole lot closer to her.

His hands slid under the back of her sweater and touched warm, soft skin. So smooth. Better than silk. His fingers eased around her. They rose up and trailed over her rib cage, and, oh, yeah, that was the edge of her bra. Close now, so—

Ding.

Oh, hell. Now he recognized the sound. The damn elevator doors. Jonas threw a fast glance over his shoulder. The doors had opened. Jamie frowned at him, two guys in suits stared with wide eyes, and a woman in red smiled.

Wrong place.

He forced his hands to slide from under Christie's sweater. Jonas slowly let her go and stepped back. He took a deep breath. He still tasted champagne and strawberries. "Christie—"

She blinked at him and shook her head. Her lips were red and glistening. *From my mouth.* Right, like he hadn't pictured this scene before. His first kiss with Christie. Except, in his fantasies, they hadn't been in an elevator and they hadn't—

"Jonas! The kids are upstairs! Santa needs to give them their gifts!"

—been surrounded by strangers and her brother. Because Daniel was closing in on them now, his turtleneck looking a little too tight around his bobbing Adam's apple.

Daniel skidded to a stop and threw his hand up, barely stopping the elevator doors from closing once more. "What are you doing, man? I need you! The employees always get to bring their kids in for the presents. You know this!" Daniel tossed him the Santa beard. Then his stare swept to his sister. "Christie, this is your favorite part!"

Because Christie designed most of the toys made by the company, she was usually front and center on the toy distribution.

"Uh, Daniel," she mumbled. "I think I'm going to—"

Daniel jumped in the elevator. "Catch the next one!" Daniel advised the folks in the lobby. He punched the button for the third floor. "I had to chase you both down three flights of stairs." The doors slid closed. "*Three flights.*" He seemed to be breathing a little hard. "Let's just get back up there and make this a merry damn night, okay?"

Jonas glanced at Christie. Her cheeks were flushed. Her lips red and plump. Her breathing was coming fast like her brother's, but it wasn't because she'd raced down three flights of stairs.

A smile curved Jonas's lips. Her gaze darted to meet his.

At that moment, the elevator music kicked in and Elvis began to sing. Jonas didn't take his eyes off Christie. Not for a moment.

When she'd first come toward him upstairs, he'd been drinking her in. Her steps had been uncertain. Her posture hesitant. He'd wanted to put her at ease.

I'm sure I have something in here for a good girl like you.

Those words hadn't put her at ease. They'd seemed to unleash something inside of her. It definitely looked like Christie Tate had a naughty side.

He couldn't wait to see what other surprises she'd been keeping from him.

CHAPTER TWO

She'd asked Jonas Kirk to sleep with her. No, she'd asked Jonas Kirk—badass police detective—to give her a really good time.

Christie was 150 percent certain the man could deliver on that good time.

She watched him from the corner of her eye. He didn't currently look all tough and kick-ass. Well, okay, he *kinda* did if you looked past the red suit and beard. He was *ho-hoing* it up with the kids as he handed out the presents that she'd organized days before.

"What was happening in that elevator?" her brother asked, and she jumped. Daniel had a tendency to sneak up on people way too much.

She forced a smile. "We were talking."

"Right. 'Cause when you talk, you make out."

Oh, no.

"I know the breakup with Charles was hard on you."

"Daniel, I—"

"I should have fired the guy, holidays or no damn holidays."

She turned her head so that she could better size up her brother. At just over six feet, he had a lean, wiry build. His face was open, warm, and handsome. "You would never fire someone at Christmas." Even he had limits.

"He hurt you." His jaw flexed. "We don't need him. I can fire him right—"

"I don't need you to fight my battles." Her gaze tracked back to Jonas. He was taller than her brother by a couple inches, and his shoulders were wider. His body stronger. She exhaled slowly. "Charles doesn't bother me. I've moved on."

A low whistle was his response. "I hope you're not moving where I *think* you're moving."

She should look away from Jonas. Yes, she should. He bent to reach into the sack again—*nice butt*.

"You know Jonas isn't the committing kind."

Her gaze snapped to Daniel.

His brows, a lighter shade than hers, rose. "Yeah, sis, I saw the hickey you left on his neck."

She'd left a hickey on him? Why, oh, why couldn't the floor just open up and swallow her?

"You *know* him, Chris. You know Jonas never stays with one woman too long."

She'd gotten that warning before. She held her brother's gaze. Heard Jonas's voice rumble as he talked to a little girl. Goose bumps rose on

Christie's arms. "I don't want forever." She'd tried to find forever before, only to get disappointed.

Daniel blinked. "Chris…"

"I'm a big girl. Trust me, I know exactly what I want." *Not what, who.* Jonas. "Stop worrying about me."

"He's my best friend! I don't want my sister and my—"

She patted his shoulder. "Stop worrying. And um, maybe lower your voice." She jerked her thumb over her shoulder. The kids were watching them now. "We've got an audience."

His teeth clicked together as he snapped his jaw closed. Turning on his heel, Daniel marched toward the giant Christmas tree.

Christie knew her cheeks were burning again, but she made herself look at their audience. An audience that included an avid Santa hunk. When she met his stare, she swore she could feel his touch. She could feel his hands—big, strong, callused—sliding against her skin. Edging up her stomach. Getting closer, so close to her breasts.

Oh, yes, she knew what she wanted. The question was…would she really be brave enough to take it? To take him?

She slipped away from the crowd. Her elbow bumped into a wall, and the pain barely registered. *Sex with Jonas.* Sure, she'd fantasized about just that very thing, over and over again.

But the real thing? Her throat dried up. Oh, jeez. It would be…She peeked back at him. Jonas was watching her. His green eyes seemed to burn. Sex with Jonas would be—

Incredible.

Because he was a man who *knew* how to give a woman a good time she'd never forget.

***

An hour later, Jonas had emptied his second sack. All the presents were gone. The kids had vanished. The staff left at Tate Toys could only be described as skeletal. As he watched, a few more folks trailed for the elevators.

Another holiday party down.

But his job wasn't finished. Not yet. Santa still had one wish to grant. Hmm. Where was his lady? His gaze swept the room. The last time he'd seen her, Christie had been trapped against that back wall.

The spot was empty now. The tree lights twinkled, throwing a mix of colors on the wall. No Christie.

He tossed his hat and the beard down next to the bag. Had she left? Turned tail and run? If she had, he knew where she lived. Not like he couldn't find her.

Just in case she hadn't fled the building, though, Jonas stalked down the hallway leading to the area known as Christie's domain. Her office was on the right side of the hallway and her lab—a giant workroom/toy construction zone—was on the left.

He went to the right. Didn't bother knocking. The door was open, so he walked in and found Christie hunched over her desk.

She looked up at him, her eyes widening. "What are you—"

He caught the doorknob and closed the door with a slow, deliberate move. *The woman needs to learn not to tease.*

Christie shot to her feet, and the chair rolled behind her with a groan of its wheels. "You were with the kids, you were—"

"Kids are gone." He stalked toward her. *I want a really good time.* She'd known she was talking to him. She must have known. Right? No way she would have said those words to another man. *I sure as hell hope she wouldn't.* "Pretty much everyone is gone but you and me."

Her small, pink tongue swiped over her lips, and he almost growled. *Still playing with fire.* Did she know how badly they could both be burned?

He put his hands on her desk and leaned across the heavy wood. "That good time you wanted..."

Her wide eyes were locked on his.

"You want it here? Now?" How far would she go? He'd caught the whispers while he was handing out the toys. It seemed Christie and her boyfriend, a dumbass called Charles, had split. A chatty chick named Lydia thought Christie was looking for some revenge sex.

He didn't enjoy being a stand-in. But he sure had dreamed about having sex with Christie. So many times. *Am I that desperate for her?* So desperate that he'd be a tool for revenge?

Um, maybe. Definite maybe. Or...just yes.

"*Here?*" Her voice was a squeak. Her gaze flew to the closed door, then back to him. "But you—"

"You didn't mean what you said?" His hands curled, forming fists on the wood. "You were just messing with me? Or maybe you thought you were just jerking around some random Santa—"

"I was *not* messing with you!" Instead of jerking back, she leaned forward and put her face temptingly close. "I knew exactly what I was saying—and I knew I was saying those words to *you!*"

Good. Excellent to know. "Then let's see about that good time." He caught her arms, pulled her even closer, and took her mouth. Because no way, no way would she still taste like—

Champagne and strawberries. Woman and lust. Everything *he* wanted for the holidays.

Oh, hell, trouble.

Christie's hands dug into his shoulders. Her mouth opened wider, and her tongue slipped right past his lips.

Revenge sex. Those stupid words whispered through his mind.

She moaned into his mouth. Two more seconds, and Jonas knew that he'd be over that desk. He wanted her so badly that nothing else mattered. Yeah, she could use him for revenge sex. Totally cool. She could—

But Christie pulled back. Spots of color stained her cheeks. Her breath came hard and fast.

"Change your mind?" Jonas rasped as he forced his body to back away. Either back away or lunge forward. He was trying to keep his control and not lunge.

"No." Her fingers touched her lips. A quick, light touch. Then she skirted around the edge of the desk and came to him.

His heart stopped.

"I didn't change my mind. I just wanted to get closer."

She was real close. In front of him. Caged between his body and the thick desk.

"This is better." She rose onto her toes again and reached for him.

Jonas caught her wrists. They felt so fragile beneath his fingers. He could feel her pulse racing along her inner wrist. "You really think you know what you're doing?"

She flinched.

What the hell? Had he just hurt her? He hadn't meant to do that. He would never, ever want to hurt Christie. He'd just wanted to make certain she was sure about the big step they were taking—

Her chin came up. "Despite what you may have heard out there, yes, I've got a pretty good idea about what I'm doing." She tried to tug her hands free.

He didn't let her go. "How did you know it was me in the Santa suit?" He'd been called in at the last minute. Daniel had originally hired another—

She laughed. "I'd know you anywhere."

"How?"

Her voice softened as she explained, "No one else has eyes like yours." Her lips curved in a half smile, revealing the faintest hint of the dimple in her right cheek. "Do you honestly think I would have just crawled onto any Santa's lap?"

She'd better not plan to be crawling on any other laps. He moved fast, and in a blink, Christie was sitting on the edge of her desk, he was between her spread thighs, and her mouth was open and eager beneath his.

Her scent surrounded him, light and feminine. Beneath the soft material of her holiday sweater, he could feel her breasts pushing at him. Her nipples were tight, hard, and he was dying to know—would they taste like strawberries, too?

Christie's hands shoved under his coat, and her palms touched his back. Her touch seemed red hot, scorching his skin.

He bit her lower lip, that full lower lip that had distracted him more times than he could count. *Christie Tate.* The woman who'd taught him long ago that smart was so very sexy.

The woman who'd barely seemed to know he existed, until tonight.

Good time, here we come. If that was what Christie wanted for Christmas, he'd make sure she had the best time of her entire life.

He pulled back just enough to grab the bottom of her sweater, then he yanked it up and over her head. Rudolph landed in the corner and—*hell.*

A black lace bra cupped her breasts. Black lace surrounding pale skin. His fingers slipped beneath the thin straps and eased the bra off her shoulders. She watched him with her bedroom eyes. Watched and waited and damn, she had beautiful breasts.

Small, but perfectly round. The nipples were dark pink. So ready for his mouth. He leaned forward. *Taste her. Taste her.* Once they crossed this line, he would never want to go back to just being *friends* with her.

She has to be certain. "How much…ah…champagne have you had tonight?" The words emerged as more rumble than anything else.

But Christie must have understood because she said, "I'm not drunk, Jonas. I know exactly what I'm doing." She paused, then asked, voice crisp, "Do you?"

Surprise rolled through him. Christie had just taunted him—challenged him. He was more than ready for that challenge. "I manage." In three minutes, he'd *manage* to make her come. That would be just the start of the fun he had planned.

His mouth closed over her left nipple. Her moan filled his ears, and oh, yeah, she tasted better than strawberries.

Her hips arched against him as he licked and sucked. *Christie fucking Tate!* Too smart, too rich, too sexy as she moaned beneath him. Her brother had never needed to tell Jonas to keep his hands off Christie. He'd known she was off-limits to him for years.

Jonas still knew, but…*screw it.*

His hands grabbed the flowing material of her skirt and yanked it up.

Hands most definitely on.

"Jonas!"

His hand was on her thigh. Soft, supple skin. So close to touching her sex. All he had to do was slide his fingers under the elastic of her panties. Would her panties be black, too? A scrap of lace to match the bra?

His gaze met hers. Passion had darkened the blue of her eyes, but wait…was that fear? Was she afraid of him? Sure, he'd pulled some dangerous undercover cases when he'd been busting ass in the Narcotics Division of the Charlotte PD. But he hadn't even gone close to Christie back in those days. He'd made a point to stay away from temptation. He'd transferred out of that department now, and . . . the woman had to know he wouldn't hurt her, right? Never in a million years would he hurt Christie. She was far too important and precious to him.

He pressed a light kiss to her lips. "Trust me."

A small furrow appeared between her brows. "That's...not easy for me."

He knew *that* about her, too.

Her gaze dropped to his hand.

His fingers began to slide up her thigh, pushing the skirt with the slow movement. "Tell me to stop," he told her. One word, and he'd back off.

One word.

Christie didn't speak.

He saw the black edge of her panties. His cock jerked—the thing was so eager for her that he ached. His hand looked too big next to her. Too rough. But he wasn't backing off. Not unless she gave the word. His index finger eased under the edge of her underwear and touched warm, wet woman.

Fuck.

Christie wanted him as much as he wanted her. His hand caught the lace, pulling too hard, and it snapped. The lace fell between them. "Spread your legs wider." His gravel-rough command.

She was still looking at his hand when she moved to obey. Her breath came faster and harder as Jonas stroked her. Her hips arched up when he pushed his index finger knuckle-deep inside her.

Watching. Watching.

Where the hell was the mistletoe when he needed it? He knew just where he wanted to kiss. Just exactly where—

The door flew open, banging against the wall, and Jonas whirled around. His first instinct was to shield her. To cover her. No one else could see Christie this way and if someone was trying to—

A tall, blond dumbass of a guy stumbled inside. "Hey, look, Christie, we really need to—"

"Get the hell out." Jonas kept his voice lethally soft. He also kept his body in front of Christie's.

The blond dumbass staggered to a stop. "What? Who are you—*Santa*?"

A choking sound came from behind Jonas.

The dumbass stepped forward even as his face flushed a dark red. "Christie! You're making out with the guy in the Santa suit?" Shock had his voice rising.

"Doing a bit more than that," Jonas told him. His voice didn't rise. Stayed soft. Lethal. Jonas lifted a brow as he studied the intruder.

The dude looked like a fish—a blond, dumbass fish—as he tried to suck in air. "You...can't...Christie and I are—"

"We're not anything anymore, Charles," Christie interrupted, her voice too calm and far too cool for a woman who'd been burning hot in Jonas's hands ten seconds ago. He glanced back at her. Her sweater was gone, but her skirt was in place. He shrugged out of his coat and wrapped her up before Charles could see—

Charles. The name clicked. Revenge sex. Hell.

This was the ex? *This tool?* Jonas straightened his shoulders and faced off against his new sworn enemy. "You're interrupting." Jonas hadn't even gotten his three minutes.

But old Charles must have gotten some kind of second wind. Suddenly he came barreling forward, and Charles launched his fist at Jonas.

Christie screamed. Jonas twisted to the side, did a fast dive, and caught the dumbass with a quick maneuver that took Charles down, face-first, onto the desk.

Jonas held Charles's hands pinned at the base of his back. The idiot kept bucking and swearing and promising to rip Jonas's head off. Right. Like that was going to happen. "Charles, this is not your Christmas." A deliberate pause. "Dumbass, you just assaulted a police officer."

CHAPTER THREE

Charles froze. The guy had finally realized he was screwed to hell and back. Good for him.

"Jonas." Christie's breathy voice filled his ears.

He focused on her. She looked mussed and sexy, and he'd been close to paradise. Until the dumbass had interrupted.

"There's been a mistake," Charles cried.

Jonas kept his eyes on Christie. She bit her lower lip, and her gaze darted between him and her ex.

"Charles..." Her breath expelled on a rush and Jonas's brows snapped together. He didn't like the look she was shooting the dumbass. "You shouldn't be here."

Damn right he shouldn't. Jonas tightened his hold around the guy's wrists.

Her ex gasped out, "Didn't know he was a cop!"

"Right. Because it's fine to assault people, as long as they aren't cops," Jonas snapped. Idiot. "Let's see if a night at the station can—"

"Jonas!" Okay, now Christie was back to calling his name. Well, not so much calling it as nearly shrieking it in horror. "You're taking him in? You're going to arrest him?"

His jaw ached, and Jonas realized he was gritting his teeth. With an effort, he forced himself to stop. "Does it matter to you?" But the real question was...*did the ex matter?* The jerk was still pinned on the desk.

Christie pulled Jonas's coat closer to her and stared back at him.

"Listen, buddy, this is a *mistake*!" Charles wailed. "I saw you with Christie and I just—"

"We're over, Charles," she stated flatly, her voice cold. *Not seeming to care so much.* "Who I'm with, who you're with—doesn't matter. That's what *over* means."

Okay, that was good enough for Jonas, and because he was suddenly feeling so generous, he eased his grip and let old Charles flop over.

Charles stared up at him with wide, gray eyes.

Jonas glared down at him. "This is your warning, asshole. You ever come at me again, and you'll find yourself in jail."

Charles's eyes darted to Christie.

Jonas stepped closer to her. "You heard the lady. *Over.* So unless you have Tate business with her, stay the hell away." He put his arm over her shoulders and pulled her against him. Territorial?

Yeah, that was him. At least where she was concerned.

Jonas finally had a chance with Christie, and no dumbass was going to ruin that for him.

Charles swallowed and tried to straighten up. "I...Christie—"

"Go, Charles. I think you're drunk. Y-you need to catch a cab and sleep this night off."

Charles gulped and then finally rushed out on wobbly legs.

The anger that fired Jonas's blood didn't cool as the door closed behind the jerk with a soft snick. "Is that what you wanted?" he demanded. *Revenge sex.* If Lydia had been right, Christie had just scored a major hit. Gotten her jealous ex to take a swing at the new man.

But Christie shook her head and, for an instant, sadness slipped over her face. "No, I-I almost had what I wanted but...maybe it's just not in the cards, huh?"

She shrugged out of his jacket and handed it back to him. Silently, she found her sweater and dressed. A light red stained her cheeks. *Embarrassment?*

Hell, he *had* been moving fast with her.

In moments, her clothes were positioned perfectly, but her hair was a bit wild, and her lips were still red and swollen.

Then she leaned up and pressed her sweet mouth against his. A kiss that was too light. Too fleeting. Her breath whispered against him. "Good night, Jonas." Her hand hovered over her stomach as she pulled away, and yeah, that was definitely fear in her eyes.

But what was she afraid of?

He watched her walk out of the office, her steps slow but sure. Jonas bent down and picked up the scrap of lace that had fallen on the floor. The panties he'd ripped off her.

He could give Christie everything she wanted, if she'd just trust him. The problem was…he didn't know if Christie was afraid of him or herself.

His fingers tightened around her panties before he shoved them into his pocket. Jonas hurried out of her office and narrowly avoided a collision in the hallway with a redhead in a dark green dress.

"Have you—have you seen Charles Crenshaw?" she asked quietly. "I think"—she sucked in a deep breath—"I think he came here looking for Christie."

"They're both gone," he told her and saw her eyes widen. *Oh, wait, shit, could this be Vicki?* Lydia had been talking about the redhead, too. Lydia had liked to talk about everyone. "They didn't leave together," Jonas clarified.

"Oh." Relief flashed across her face.

Right. Whatever. She could deal with the dumbass. Charles wasn't a priority for him anymore.

Only Christie mattered.

***

The snow had just started to fall when Christie heard the knock at her door. She'd been staring out the back window, thinking about—

who else?—Jonas and what an idiot she'd been the previous night.

Running away. Nice. Smooth.

Sometimes, it seemed like she'd spent years running from him. No, not from him. From herself.

The knock came again, harder. She frowned. Okay, usually the delivery driver just knocked once and left her package on the doorstep. Maybe he needed her signature this time? She hurried to the foyer and peeked out the peephole.

Not the delivery driver.

Jonas stood on the other side of the door. Her hand slapped against the wood. *Oh, damn.* Her fingers were shaking as she fumbled with the lock and the doorknob. *Don't screw this up again. Try to be cool. Confident. Act like you're a woman who's had lots of sex. Lots of great sex on desks and heck, everywhere!*

He'd almost made her come on top of a desk. Her knees jiggled as she yanked open the door. "Jonas!" Her smile felt huge on her face.

He stared at her a moment, then blinked and shook his head.

Her smile dimmed. Why was he looking at her that way? Snowflakes had fallen onto his battered black leather jacket—a jacket that made his golden skin look darker and his black, windblown hair even sexier.

Sexy. That was the word that always sprang to mind when she thought of Jonas. Jonas with the wicked green eyes and slightly crooked nose, courtesy of a bar fight he'd broken up when he'd been a rookie cop.

His lips—the top a little thin, the bottom perfectly bitable—curved as he watched her.

She cleared her throat. "What are you...um, doing here?" The words were a little too high. Not the confident air she'd been hoping to achieve.

His black brows rose. "Mind if I come in?" A puff of white appeared before his mouth. "Damn cold out here."

Oh, yes, right. Of course. She opened the door wider. Jonas stomped his boots on her mat, then crossed the threshold and immediately made her feel that her doorway was too small. He was too big. He was—

He had a package in his hands. A small, red box with a dark green bow. "I brought you something."

He'd never given her a present before. Not once, and sometimes, it felt like she'd known him forever. Known him, wanted him, had too much champagne and finally asked for her secret desire.

Christie pushed the door closed behind them. Her eyes were on the present. It looked small and innocent in his big, gloved hands. Except there was nothing innocent about him. She knew that.

"Don't worry," Jonas told her as he flashed a smile that revealed his perfect white teeth. "It's not going to bite you."

But I will. The words seemed to hang in the air as she gaped at him. Christie gulped and stepped forward to take the present. "It's...uh...not Christmas yet." Not for another week. They'd had the party at Tate Toys last night because it had been Friday night. The perfect opportunity for a party because not many folks had to get up early the next day. And lots of their employees were taking the next week off for the holiday.

"Anything wrong with an early present between friends?" His gloved fingers brushed hers as she took the gift. A lick of heat seemed to shoot right through her body.

She was holding the present too tightly. "Is that what we are? Friends?" She tasted the word. Jonas had been on the cusp of her life for so long. When she'd transferred to Duke University, he and Daniel had already been roommates. Jonas had treated her like a kid sister, too. She'd been crazy about him. One look in those green eyes...

She shook the present. Didn't hear anything.

Jonas shrugged out of his coat and hung it on the rack. His gloves landed on the entranceway table. "We could be friends." His head cocked to the right as he studied her. "We could be more."

Lovers.

"Don't crush the box," he advised softly, and she realized her hold had turned into a death grip.

Her breath expelled slowly and her fingers relaxed a little.

Jonas strolled into her den. He whistled lightly. "That's some tree."

A bit of the tension eased from her body and her smile came back as she followed him. "Thanks. Daniel helped me get it inside." The tree brushed her sixteen-foot ceiling. "It took me two days to decorate it but—"

"But you love Christmas, so you had one hell of a time, right?" He'd turned toward her. His eyes gleamed as he studied her.

"Right." Softly spoken.

"You're the one who decorates Tate Toys every year, aren't you?"

How did he—

"Daniel has told me how much you love this time of year." His gaze dipped to her jingle bell sweater. "And it's kinda...easy to see."

She lifted the present. "I-I'll just...put this under the tr—tree." Dammit, she hated her nervous stutter. Just when she thought she'd had the thing under control, Jonas stared at her and—wham, it was back. She sucked in a breath and tried again, "I-I'll just put this under the tree with the—"

"I'd rather you opened it now."

Why did his voice sound like sex? Well, not *like* sex, but that rumble made her think of sex. Of sheets and darkness, of a strong body surrounding hers and of a growl telling her to—

"Actually, before you open it, we need to talk." He stalked toward her. The fire crackled behind him and sent a blaze of warmth into the room. "Over the years, we haven't done much *talking*, have we?"

She shook her head, aware that her heartbeat had kicked way up.

"I've done a lot of watching you." His stare was on her. His hand lifted and brushed a lock of hair back from her cheek. "Sure as hell a lot of fantasizing."

What?

"But not a whole lot of actual talking."

Christie tried to clear her throat, then said, "You never...seemed much interested in talking."

After he'd graduated, he'd joined the police force. He'd fast-tracked to the narcotics division then—

"When I was undercover"—he shook his head—"you didn't want to be around me."

"That's not true! I—" *I've always wanted to be near you.*

"I spent my days with criminals. I lived their lives." His hand dropped. "I didn't *want* you to know the things I did. Didn't want any part of that world to touch you."

He'd cared? Her stomach tightened. "I...didn't realize you'd even—" *Noticed me.* Okay, she couldn't say that. She had her pride. But the years had trickled away, and he'd spared her the briefest of greetings when their paths had crossed. She hadn't thought he'd noticed her as a woman, and she certainly hadn't realized Jonas was interested in her.

Until last night.

"Always the princess," he murmured, and his eyes raked around her home, "safe in the castle." His focus came back to her. He closed the distance between them.

She stiffened. Yes, the Tate family had money. A lot of it. But she wasn't some spoiled debutante who didn't know the meaning of work, and she wasn't some weak-willed woman who'd break at the first sign of a bleak reality. "I don't live in a castle. I live in the real world. I work every day. I earn my own money, I—"

He kissed her. A light, sensual brush of his lips that halted her words and stirred the need that had built within her.

"I know what you do," he murmured as he pulled back a bit from her. "I know so much more than you think."

Her brows lifted even as she licked her lips. *Trying to taste him.* She had it bad. A crush that should have ended years ago, but now—

I know he wants me. There was no holding back for her.

"It's not about revenge, is it?" Jonas asked. "I don't think it ever was."

He'd lost her. Totally. What revenge? "Uh, Jonas—"

"I heard one of your coworkers last night. The folks who saw us in the elevator spread word pretty fast about what we were doing."

Making out in that tight elevator. His body pressed to hers. His tongue in her mouth. His hands all over her. Hers on him.

More, please. "Ah, how does that mean I want revenge against you?" She was still confused.

"Not me, baby. Your ex. The dumbass who came barreling into your office like he had some kind of right to be there, with you."

A surprised laugh broke from her lips. "Charles? You think I want revenge on Charles?" She shook her head but never eased her hold on the package. "My brother owns the business, remember? If I wanted revenge, Charles would be out looking for a new job."

His gaze measured her. "But you don't work that way."

No, she didn't. "You heard what I told him. Charles and I are over." She forced a shrug. "End of story." The minute Jonas's lips had brushed hers, she'd barely even been able to remember Charles's touch.

"Good to hear." His stare dropped to the box. "Got a deal to offer you."

A deal?

"You told me what you wanted last night."

Ah, yes. Champagne and false Christmas courage. A dangerous mix. "I told you but, um, you were the one who followed me." She had to point that part out. It wasn't like she'd forced him to do anything. "You came after me. You kissed *me*. Both in the elevator and in my office."

"And I plan to do a hell of a lot more than just kiss you." His voice roughened.

Christie rocked forward.

His eyes narrowed. "You want your good time? Well, I can promise you the best sex you've ever had."

She locked her knees. "Awful s-sure of yourself." Since she'd had three lovers who'd delivered only average sex, and one other guy who'd been *really* disappointing, odds were high that Jonas could make good on his promise. Not that she'd tell him and his ego that info.

"I'm sure of you," he stated. "When I touched you..."

Her nipples tightened. Her body seemed to *yearn*.

"You went up in flames. Since I'm going to do a lot more touching, I know just how hot your body is going to burn for mine." His eyes glittered. "I can give you what you want for Christmas. Exactly what you want."

She knew he could. "Great sex, no strings," she whispered. *Not boring, not with him.*

The faint lines around his eyes tightened.

She'd heard her brother talk often about Jonas and his women over the years. Jonas and his flavor of the week. Daniel had been right when he warned her last night. Jonas wasn't a commitment kind of guy. He never settled down long with anyone. "Not forever." The words slipped out.

He gave a hard nod. "Just sex."

Christie's chin lifted even as her heart slammed into her chest. She'd been brave last night. She could pull on the mask again. "The best we've *both* ever had." No stutter.

His breath came harder as his nostrils flared, almost as if he had just pulled in her scent. "Open the box."

Her fingers jerked at the bow. Ripped away the paper. She fumbled with the box top, opened it, and found—

A small scrap of lace. She lifted it up, and the dark red lace dangled from her fingertips. *Panties.* He'd given her panties. Really sexy, really hot panties that wouldn't cover *anything*.

A wild woman would love this gift. She'd laugh, then wear those panties and nothing else for her lover. A wild woman would do just that.

What about a good girl pretending to be wild? What would she do?

Christie dropped the box, but kept the lace in her hand.

His eyes were on her face. He seemed even bigger now. Or maybe her room was getting smaller.

"I tore your panties last night."

Oh, God. Heat rose in her cheeks. Yes, he'd torn them, and she'd *left them* in her office. Smooth.

"Figured the least I could do was give you a new pair." His hand lifted and tangled with hers. "A pair for you to wear just for me."

Jonas Kirk was standing in front of her, promising her great sex, and giving her sexy underwear. This scene was really similar to a dream she'd had last week.

His head tilted toward her. "You up for this?" he dared her.

What? Did he think she was all talk? That she'd turn away when things got too hot? Hadn't he realized she was desperate for the heat? She was sick of being cold.

"Stay here," she told him. Even to her own ears, her voice sounded too husky. She eased around him. Christie forced herself to walk, nice and slow, and added a little roll to her hips as she left him. *Watch me, watch me.*

At her bedroom door, Christie glanced back just in time to catch his gaze on her ass. More confident, she threw him a smile.

Then she closed the door and shut him out, right before her knees buckled.

CHAPTER FOUR

Jonas sucked in a deep gulp of air. The fresh scent of pine filled his nostrils even as the taste of Christie stayed on his tongue. He rolled his shoulders and paced toward the glittering tree. Okay, so he hadn't screwed things up too badly. She was still interested in him. Well, maybe not *him*, but in having *sex* with him. No-strings, no-promises sex.

He'd sure had plenty of that in his life.

The door creaked open behind him. He swung around and took a hard punch to the gut—or at least, it sure as shit felt like he did.

Christie stood in the doorway, her long black hair loose around her face, her deep blue bedroom eyes tempting him...and she was naked.

His cock shoved against the front of his jeans, and he lunged toward her.

"The panties fit," she told him, her cheeks a little red, and he managed to jerk his gaze off her breasts—absolutely beautiful breasts with tight pink nipples—and he saw that she was wearing the scrap of lace he'd given her.

So *not* completely naked. Still so sexy he hurt.

The lace rode low on her round, perfect hips. Hips that he'd grab and hold tight while he drove into her. Hips that—

Her eyebrows lowered. "Jonas, is everything—"

"Perfect. Everything is perfect." He took two steps and stood before her. Stood and just stared. *Damn.* Her skin was so smooth. Smooth and creamy and he had to touch her. His hands lifted and skimmed down her shoulders. She shivered.

She wants me, just as much as I want her.

"The bedroom," Christie began. "It's behind me and—"

He shook his head, caught her right hand with his and pulled her with him. Not toward her bedroom but back across the room. Back toward the glittering Christmas tree. A thick rug was spread between the tree and the fireplace. The rug would do nicely for what he had in mind.

"Are you going to—to take off your clothes?" Christie asked. Her voice was husky. Sensual. A little hesitant. "Y-you should—"

He gently pushed her down onto the rug. "Not yet."

Her breath blew out in a rush. He lowered onto his knees. Stared more and realized he had to touch. Not just with his hands. With his mouth.

Jonas knew exactly where he wanted to start.

"Jonas, are you—"

Her words ended in a gasp when he licked her breast. She arched up toward him. *Just as responsive as last night.* So, no, he hadn't been imaging things. Hadn't made it better in his memory. One touch—*fire.*

He spread his lips wider and took her breast into his mouth. Tasted. Sucked.

Jonas heard the rasp of her breath. Her hands rose and locked around his shoulders. The faint edge of her nails bit through his shirt.

"Easy," he whispered as he lifted his head.

But his "good" girl shook her head. "I don't want easy. I want you." Her hand went to the buckle of his belt. "And I want you now, Jonas." Demanding.

She unhooked the buckle, went for the snap and the zipper—

He backed away from her. "Not yet." He wasn't going to let the first time be too fast or too hard. He'd promised her the best sex she'd ever had, and he was damn well going to deliver on that promise.

Even if it killed him.

"Spread your legs," he ordered, his voice dropping to a growl.

Her legs shifted on the rug, then parted.

Jonas realized his zipper was probably making a permanent imprint on his dick. He was so turned on by her that he hurt.

He positioned his body between her legs, letting his jeans brush her thighs, and giving him a perfect view of her body.

She stared at him. Her eyes were wide. Her lips were parted, and Christie's pink tongue darted just behind her teeth. *Waiting.*

He stretched over her and took her mouth. Jonas kissed her long and deep and let his tongue take and claim. He took her mouth the way he'd soon be taking her body.

Mine.

He'd make sure she didn't forget him, not any time soon. Not ever.

Jonas licked his way down her neck. When he came to the spot just under her left ear, her hips rocked up against him. He stilled. Then licked her again.

Another fast rock.

So his lady had a sweet spot. He bet she had more, and he was ready to find them all. But first...His fingers eased under the scrap of lace. *Sweetest spot of all.* He found her already wet and so incredibly hot. A moan trembled in her throat as he stroked her.

He bit lightly on her neck, and when her hips arched again, he let his index finger dip inside her.

She shuddered beneath him. *Fuck, yes.*

But...not yet. Jonas pulled his hand from her and kissed his way down her body. Jonas took his time with her breasts, licking and sucking those tight nipples. He loved the feel of her nipples on his tongue. The taste—still strawberries—still drove him crazy.

Her thighs lifted and squeezed him. "I can't— more!"

He'd give her more. He'd give her everything she could handle and everything she couldn't.

The curve of her stomach tempted his mouth. When his lips pressed just under her belly button, she gasped his name. Another sensual spot. A weakness for her, a temptation for him. He bit her, then sucked the skin. Jonas marked the area, and she trembled beneath him even as her hands clutched his shoulders.

His head lowered more. He licked down her abdomen. His breath blew over the lace.

"Jonas…"

Sweat beaded his brow as he looked up at her.

Lust and need burned in her eyes. "Jonas, I want you to—"

Taste me.

The words hung in the air between them. But she bit her lip and her gaze dropped.

He blew against the lace once more. Her hips lifted helplessly. "You want me to touch you again?" he asked.

A jerky nod.

His fingers caressed her through the lace. He traced lightly over her sex, and the lace grew damp. Christie was ready for him. He was insane for her.

He lowered his mouth to the lace. Jonas kissed her through the fabric and felt her body go bow tight. It wouldn't take much to push her into a climax. Not much at all.

His fingers pulled on the lace. His control slipped away. It broke from him as her scent teased him and—

And the lace ripped.

"Buy you more," he promised as he tossed the panties aside. He put his mouth on her and tasted her like he'd wanted to do for so long. When his tongue pressed against the center of her need, Christie came. He felt the orgasm roll through her. She shuddered beneath him and whispered his name.

Jonas figured that was a good start. And he *was* only starting. He didn't stop. Wasn't close to stopping. He tasted and he took and he got drunk off her. He would never get enough of Christie. Every lick had him wanting so much more. When she came against his mouth a second time, he growled his pleasure. *Love the way she tastes.*

"Jonas! Jonas, what about you—"

He pushed away from her. The drum of his heartbeat filled his ears. It took two seconds to ditch his jeans. Two more to slide on his condom and then he was plunging into her. Driving as deep as he could go. The ripples of her release teased his cock, and he drove into her, faster, harder.

His hands caught hers. Their fingers threaded together. Their eyes locked.

Thrust.

So blue, so dark...her eyes held his. Her gaze had gone wild with lust.

The tree lights glittered down on them. Shining bright.

Thrust.

Her legs wrapped around his hips and held on tight. Her ankles pressed against him, and she met him, thrust for thrust. He drove into her. Deeper. Harder.

"Jonas!"

He climaxed with her—and it was fucking incredible.

***

Eventually, they made it to her bed. Had sex again. Slow and tender this time. Christie was pretty sure there wasn't an inch of her body that Jonas hadn't kissed. She felt so *good*. No, better than good. Better than she'd ever felt in her entire life.

"You sure know how to deliver on a promise," she murmured as her hand trailed down the muscular expanse of his chest.

His eyes opened, and he turned his head toward her.

"That was definitely the best sex I've had," she told him. Her voice was very, very serious.

His lips parted, but she leaned forward and kissed him before Jonas could speak. *Don't tell me any lies. Don't tell me I'm the best. Don't.*

Jonas wasn't like her. Sheltered didn't enter his vocabulary. She knew the guy had been with more sexual partners than she had. She didn't want to hear lies from him. Not now, not ever.

"Another rule for us," she whispered as she eased back and smiled at him. Christie smiled so he wouldn't see that it mattered to her. "No lies, okay?" She'd had plenty of those from her other lovers.

From Benjamin, her first lover. He'd sworn he loved her, but really, he'd just loved her family's money. Yes, she'd found out about that. Thanks to Jonas. When Ben had started talking about an engagement, Daniel had used Jonas to dig up background information on the guy. It hadn't taken long before they found out about Ben's debts. When her dad had offered Ben ten grand to walk, well, Ben hadn't just walked. He'd run.

And now the dust was still settling from Charles. Another lover who'd lied. Another mistake.

"I've never lied to you." Jonas's deep voice rumbled beside her.

No, he hadn't.

"Then let's not start." Her hand stilled on his chest. "I don't want you to promise me forever." Ben had done that. Forever had lasted two months. "I don't want you to tell me I'm the love of your life." Ronnie had done that. He'd told her she was great. Wonderful. They'd had sex—the sex that had just been...bad. The great love affair had ended fast. "I don't want to hear sweet words that don't really mean anything."

His hand caught hers. "Didn't realize you were so cynical, Christie."

She laughed. "I didn't realize I was, either."

He brought her hand to his lips. "Then let's go ahead and clear the air."

Her brows rose.

"I'm not sleeping with you because I want a slice of the Tate money." He bit the pad of her palm. "Yeah, I remember that dick Ben. He thought he'd hit pay dirt when he found you in college."

Had she really been so naive? It hurt to remember. But Jonas was wrong about one thing. It hadn't been college. She'd been in grad school then. "I never agreed to marry him." She hadn't loved him. Even then, she'd—

"I didn't want Ben using you. I know it pissed you off the way that scene went down." Another bite, then a lick of his tongue. "Daniel and I wanted you safe."

"And here I didn't think you'd ever cared." She tried to sound flippant.

His hold tightened on her hand. "There's a lot you don't know." His breath feathered over her fingers. "When I'm with you, I'm with you. There's no one else for me." He paused. "Or for you. I'm not the sharing kind."

"Neither am I." But how long would they have together? Just how long would her wish last?

"This holiday is mine," he told her gruffly. Jonas moved even closer to her. "You made your wish, and this year, you'll get it—me—as many times as you can handle."

His lips were so close to hers. "I think I can handle quite a lot." Everything.

This holiday. She'd take him, she'd take the pleasure he gave, and when the new year came...well, she'd deal with the end then.

For now, she'd deal with the big, bad, sexy detective in her bed. She'd enjoy every moment they had. Christie parted her lips and kissed her Santa Claus.

***

The beeping woke her hours later. A long, steady pulse of sound. She threw out her hand, reaching for her alarm clock, and her hand hit warm, male flesh.

"It's mine," a deep voice rumbled.

Her eyes flew open. and she saw a dark shadow pull away from her and rise from the bed.

What—The grogginess vanished as her memory flooded back.

Jonas. Sex. Pleasure.

Christie blinked a few times. Those first few moments after waking were always a little fuzzy for her.

But—*what* was his? What had he been talking about?

"North and Byron. Right. I'll be there in fifteen minutes." His voice didn't sound so sleepy. He seemed completely awake. Aware. And...a little distant. Christie squinted as she tried to force her eyes to adjust to the darkness. Jonas was on a phone. That was what the buzzing had been— his phone ringing.

She sat up in bed and pulled the covers to her chest. A glance at the alarm clock told her it was only a little past four a.m.

Callused fingertips brushed her cheek. "I have to go."

She jerked a bit, surprised to find him so close.

His hand dropped.

She reached out at once as she tried to fumble and catch his hand. "What's happened?"

"Baby, you don't want to know."

She found his hand and held tight. "I told you. I'm *not* some princess in a castle. I can handle your life."

He exhaled, the sound a rough sigh that drifted to her. "A man shot his wife and turned the gun on himself. They need me at the scene ASAP." He pulled away from her, and she missed him instantly. "You know that I transferred to homicide."

No more undercover missions for him. Daniel had told her that. But Jonas still dealt with blood and death every day. *Every night.*

Clothes rustled. He was dressing. He'd be leaving soon. She jumped from the bed and rammed her thigh into the nightstand that she'd *known* was there. So why hit it? That was just what she always did in the dark. "Wait!" Christie tugged the sheet with her and rushed to meet him at the bedroom door.

"I have to go. It's my job. You know—"

"Come back when your work's done." The words slipped out. She didn't want him going back home alone after this case. His voice had been too cold when he told her about the crime. Too emotionless. It wasn't a case that didn't matter to him. No, this one would matter too much.

Jonas kept saying he knew more about her than she realized. She knew a heck of a lot more about him, too. Far more than he suspected.

She flipped on the lights and saw his face. The tight lines. The hard mask. "Come back to me when your work's done," she said again. "I'll be here. I don't care what time it is." *I'll be waiting for you.*

"I have to secure the scene. Talk to witnesses. I have to—"

"I don't care how long it takes. I'll be here."

He kissed her. Too fast, too hard, and she knew he had to go. Christie followed him to the garage door. He'd pulled his car inside earlier.

She watched him leave. When the garage door opened, she saw that it had started to snow again. Soft, drifting snowflakes floated in the air.

She pulled the sheet tighter around her body and felt the chill seep into her bones.

A man shot his wife and turned the gun on himself. A horrible crime. So terrible. So brutal. And it was Jonas's worst nightmare. She knew it. After he'd dug into Benjamin's past, she'd wanted a little vengeance. So she'd dug into Jonas's life. She'd found out his life wasn't nearly as perfect as she'd thought.

Not even close.

When Jonas had been sixteen, he'd come home to find his mother's dead body. She'd been killed by a man she knew and loved—Jonas's father.

"Come back to me," Christie whispered, but Jonas was already gone.

CHAPTER FIVE

He didn't come back. Christie stared at the clock on her bedside once more. Ten p.m. There'd been no call all day long. No call and no sign of Jonas as the hours had slipped by.

She should go to bed. Okay, she was *in* bed, but she should go to sleep. She needed to stop thinking about him. Stop worrying. Only she couldn't because she'd seen a picture of him years before when she had done her vengeance digging. A grainy photo of him at his parents' funeral. He'd been alone at the funeral. Standing all by himself.

She shoved back the covers. She'd be damned if she left him alone now. She wouldn't—

Something thudded against her front door. Her heart raced even as she jumped to her feet. Thudded? No, wait that was knocking—*pounding*—at her door.

Christie ran down the hallway. She almost fell when her socks slid across the foyer floor. But she made it to the door and pressed her eye to the peephole. The porch light fell across Jonas's stark face.

She wrenched open the door as fast as she could.

No present waited in his hands this time. No smile lit his face. He stared at her with glittering eyes. The snow had turned into icy rain and it pelted down behind him. She grabbed his hand. "Come in, Jonas! Hurry!"

He let her pull him across the threshold. "It's late. I shouldn't be here."

"This is *exactly* where you should be." She shoved off his coat.

His gaze dropped. "I worked the case all day. I stopped at my place a few minutes ago to change. I should have"—his hands flexed, balling into fists—"should have just stayed there. Not intruded here. You don't need to—"

"I need you." More than she'd realized. So much more. "I'm glad you're here."

His hands caught hers and held too tight.

"Jonas." Her chest hurt. "It's okay, I know—"

He kissed her. Not the sexy, hungry kisses he'd given her before. The kisses that had teased and tormented and made her want more. No, this was different. He was different.

The kiss was rough. Demanding. His tongue drove into her mouth even as he lifted her into his arms. The bite of his fingers stung her skin, but she didn't stop him. She wrapped her arms around him and held on as tightly as she could, her grip as fierce as his.

They made it to the bedroom. He put her on the bed and stripped off his clothes while watching her with his too-bright stare.

Christie yanked off her T-shirt and shimmied out of her shorts and panties.

He grabbed her ankle and tugged her to the edge of the bed.

"Can't wait this time." There was a dangerous edge to his words. Tension held his body tight. A muscle flexed in his jaw. *"Can't wait."*

She parted her thighs wider for him. "I don't want you to wait." She'd told him before that slow and easy wasn't what she needed from him. "I just want you."

"Careful what you wish for," he muttered. He had a condom on already. She hadn't even seen him pull out the packet.

He plunged into her, driving so deep in a thrust that stole her breath. She'd said she could handle it, handle him, but she hadn't realized...

Her hands pushed against his shoulders.

Jonas froze. His gaze held hers. Rage boiled in his stare. Lust.

Fear?

"Christie..."

She rolled her hips beneath him as she tried to find a better position. Then his hand was stroking her. Pressing in just the right spot. His mouth went to her neck, and when his tongue licked beneath her ear, a moan slipped past her lips and the tension eased away from her body.

This was Jonas. She could trust him. He'd keep her safe. He'd give her pleasure, always.

He withdrew. Thrust deep again. Still hard, still wild, but she was ready for him. Her hands held tight to his shoulders. The bed shook beneath them. The headboard banged into the wall.

More. Harder. Deeper.

His teeth bit lightly against her throat. His hands caught her legs, and he lifted them high, even as he drove into her. Again and again.

The orgasm hit her. It swept over Christie on a fierce wave of pleasure that had her tensing and digging her nails into his flesh. His head shot up, and he stared down at her with eyes that blazed.

Too much lust. Too much need.

"Christie..." He took her mouth. Kissed her as he came.

She held him as close as she could and felt the frantic, thudding beat of her heart.

Her heart...or his?

In the aftermath, they didn't speak. He pulled away from her when she wanted to hold him close. The movement made her chest ache, but she didn't say a word. They were just about sex, right? Not emotions.

Just sex.

So why did she blink back tears when he withdrew from her? Why was she swiping those teardrops away as fast as she could while he was in the bathroom?

Christie pressed her damp hand against the bed in an attempt to wipe away the evidence, and she hurriedly slipped under the covers. The sex had been intense. Almost too intense. The climax had hit her when she hadn't expected that much pleasure. It had dug through her, hollowing out her body until she felt like only a thin shell remained.

The lights clicked off, and the room plunged into darkness. She was grateful for the darkness. It was so easy to hide in the shadows.

Was that why Jonas had turned off the lights?

The bed dipped when he climbed in beside her. She wanted to roll toward him, but—yes, dammit—fear held her back. She didn't move at all.

But he reached for her. His fingers softly trailed down her arm. "Did I hurt you?"

What? "No, of course not!"

"I'm sorry. I was rough. I shouldn't have—"

She rolled toward Jonas and grabbed him. "You didn't break me. You didn't even bruise me." But she might have bruised him. There at the end, she'd held on as fiercely as she could.

One of his hands lifted. His fingers traced her cheek. Her breath caught. *No, don't let him feel the wetness from—*

"Were you crying?" His voice was gruff. "Jesus, Christie, I *did* hurt you!"

"No, you did not physically hurt me. I promise." But...she'd hurt when he pulled away. Hurt when she remembered that it was all just a fantasy. *Only sex.* She had to get her emotions under control. Christie released a slow breath. "I was worried about you." It seemed safe to make the confession in the dark.

Silence. Tension hummed in the air. "No need, baby. It's my job. I take down killers every day."

But not killers who hit so close to home. Suddenly, she wanted to break through his shell and force him to open up to her. "I know what happened."

"Yeah." Jonas eased away from her. *Again.* "An asshole high on drugs shot his wife and then turned the gun on himself when the cops showed up. A wasted—"

"I don't mean today." Her tongue felt too thick in her mouth, and her heart still beat too fast. "I mean...b-before...with y-your parents." Of course, her stutter would be back. No way to hide her nerves.

The silence was painful. Then he jumped out of the bed, and light exploded in the room when he hit the lamp.

He stared down at her. Naked, face hard, eyes narrowed, Jonas demanded, "What the hell are you talking about?"

It was a good thing she'd already pulled up the sheet. "I-I know what happened to your family." *And how hard today must have been. So hard that when you came back—*

"How?" he bit out.

Ah, now this part was dicey. "Jonas..."

"Did you call Daniel when I left for the case? Did he tell you that shit about—"

"I've never talked to Daniel about this." She took a breath. A deep one. *No stutter.*

"Then how did you find out? Who've you been talking to?"

She tucked the covers around her legs. "I found out years ago. Right after you discovered that Ben was a gold digger." Her shoulders lifted and fell in a shrug that was anything but careless. "You tore into my life, so—"

"So you thought it was only fair to tear into mine." He spun away and yanked on his jeans. "I did that to protect you! Your father and brother asked for my help! I'd just started working as a cop. We were all worried—"

"I know." But back then, she'd only been angry. Hurt. *Humiliated.* The family had bought off her lover. They hadn't tried to talk to her. They'd just tried to run her life.

Not anymore.

"How? How did you find out?"

She blinked. "It wasn't hard, Jonas." Everything was public record. "I knew you'd been born in Athens, Georgia. I just searched through some of the newspapers online and tried to find a reference to you."

"Because you wanted some payback?"

"I saw an article about the deaths of your parents. A picture of you at the funeral."

He stopped pacing near the foot of her bed. "All this time, you've known?"

She gave a quick nod.

"Why didn't you say something?"

I didn't know what to say. The last thing she'd wanted was to hurt him. *Sorry* just hadn't seemed to cover the situation. "Why didn't you?" she asked instead, her voice soft.

The laugh that broke from him held no humor. "We already covered that you and I didn't *talk* much." He strode closer to her as he edged around the bed. "You knew and you still came to me?"

She didn't understand.

His hand lifted as if he were going to touch her cheek. But his fingers fisted and fell away. "I knew I shouldn't have touched you."

Now that was bull. "You're the man who *should* have touched me." *Long ago*. It was late and the words were weak, but she continued, "I-I'm sorry about your parents. That must have been terrible for you. I can't even imagine what it must have been like—"

His head snapped up. He glared at her with glittering eyes and a clenched jaw. The angry mask was back in full effect.

Her chin notched up, too. She clutched the sheet, tucked it under her arms, and climbed out of the bed. She huffed out a hard breath and grabbed him. "I *know* I don't understand how it felt, okay? But I am sorry you had to go through that pain. No one should ever see—"

"The bloody bodies of their parents?" His lips twisted. "I see bodies every day. It's my job."

"That wasn't your job."

"*That's* why I do my job. *That's* why I became a cop."

Yes, she'd thought as much. The newspaper report had said...

"He was on drugs, Christie. My old man was so strung out he barely recognized his own family. My mom had kicked him out. She was trying to make a better life for us."

A life that had ended too soon. That fist was back, squeezing her heart too tightly. She didn't let Jonas go. Christie kept her hands on him. Her eyes stayed locked with his.

"He broke in. By the looks of the place, I know he came looking for money. He trashed everything. My mom—she must have been trying to stop him when he—he—" His mouth snapped closed. But she knew what came next.

Sixteen. He'd been through so much at such a young age.

"The cops told me it looked like he tried to help her. He even managed to make a 9-1-1 call. Hell, maybe the asshole finally realized what the hell he'd done. He called the ambulance for her, and then he killed himself. One shotgun blast to the head."

Jonas had arrived before the ambulance. He'd been the one to find the bodies.

She wrapped her arms around his neck and let the sheet drop. The sheet didn't matter. He mattered. Her lips pressed against his neck.

"You should be telling me to get the hell out now." His arms weren't around her. His body was held stiffly. Too tense and hard. "My dad was an addict who killed my mom. You know what kind of bloodline I've got. You don't need to be letting me touch—"

"Shut up, Jonas." Now he was pissing her off. "You're not your dad." She angled her head back and stared into his eyes. "You're a good man, a good cop. You just got a real crap hand dealt to you."

His eyes widened.

"Now get back in bed," she ordered him, hoping her voice sounded tough and strong. Hoping he didn't notice that her hands were shaking. The new Christie she was trying to be—the wild one who went after what she wanted—well, she wouldn't let her man walk away. Not after the hell day he'd had. She wouldn't wilt under his hot, green stare. Wouldn't flinch from the pain in his past. No, the new Christie would be tougher than all that.

Jonas slowly climbed back into bed with her. Her breath eased out when his head touched the pillow. *Good.*

She hit the lights and plunged them back into darkness because she could only keep the image of the new Christie up for so long.

Jonas's arms came around her. He pulled her against his body. A warm, strong body. A strong lover. One who was hers for a brief time. *No commitments.* It was just supposed to be about sex. And just sex meant no emotions.

So why the hell was she blinking away tears again and hoping that none of the drops fell onto his arm?

The cops told me it looked like he tried to help her.

The new Christie might be good at bluffing, but underneath that facade, she was the same woman. A woman who cared too much. A woman who had one very big weakness.

A weakness who was holding her in his arms. Cradling her, close to his heart.

CHAPTER SIX

He was in trouble. Jonas stared at the small green box in his hand and wondered how the hell something as simple as no-strings sex could become so complicated.

Ah, but then, the answer was obvious. Christie was involved—and the woman tended to complicate everything.

"Hey, man, you shouldn't have!" A hairy hand snatched the present out of Jonas's grasp. He shot to attention—too late—and saw his partner, Scotty McKenzie, clutching the present. "I didn't get nothin' for you!" Scotty declared, his voice too loud.

Jonas shook his head. "Trust me, man, that's not your size."

Scotty blinked, then laughed, a deep, rumbling laugh that sounded like a train engine. "Then I'm guessing it belongs to the lady you were so hot to see last night. The one who had you smelling like a strawberry patch when you came to the crime scene."

Yeah, her smell had been on him, and he'd liked it. It had helped to combat the stench of death all over the place.

"Didn't even know you had a lady." Scotty threw his body in the wobbly desk chair. "I mean, not one that you stayed with longer than a weekend." He tossed the box back to Jonas.

Jonas caught it in one hand. He'd already practically stayed the weekend with Christie. And, at first, he'd done just what he promised. *One hell of a good time.*

The last thing he'd expected was to get a call about a scene like that, with *her* there.

He put the box on the desk and ran a hand over his face. When he'd gone back to her place, his control had been shot. Rage had ridden him. The fury that he'd held close for so many years.

He'd been desperate to get back to Christie. He'd known she'd help him banish the past and forget the blood. He'd also known he was walking a very thin line, but he'd gone back anyway.

Call him a damn moth to the flame.

He'd been on her too fast. Too hard. The sex had been rough and wild. But she'd opened her body to him. Held tight. Changed the fury that rode him to passion.

Good time? No, that didn't even come close to describing what he had with her.

Then she'd blown his world apart with her little confession. His darkest, most painful secret. And all these years she'd known...

"Hey, man!" Scotty rolled his chair forward. "You with me?"

Jonas blinked.

"What?" Scotty's lips lifted in his usual crooked grin. "You realizing you already spent too much time with this one? Gotta be careful, she'll think you're getting attached."

His gaze darted to the box.

"Tell you what." The chair wheels squeaked as Scotty rolled ever closer. "I'll do you a favor since it's the holidays. You don't want to leave some poor woman on her own at this time of the year." He threw his arms out wide. "Since I'm a generous, bighearted kind of guy, I'll take her off your hands."

"The hell you will." Jonas's response came out bullet fast.

Scotty blinked. His smile kicked up even more and he said, "Ah, like that, is it?"

Shit, no. "She and I have a deal." Not just a weekend thing. "The holidays are mine." After that, reality could come back.

In reality, he and Christie weren't—

Scotty whistled. "You've got it bad."

Maybe. He opened his mouth to say—

"Jonas?"

He whirled at the sound of that husky voice. A voice he'd never in a million freaking years expected to hear in the bullpen at the police station. But there she was. Christie stood just inside the doorway, right under the gold garland Scotty had stapled up yesterday. Her black hair hung loosely around her face. Her eyes were on him—wide, blue, and welcoming—and her lips were lifted in a warm smile.

"Oh, man," Scotty whispered. His voice was a little shocked. A *lot* interested. "I could *so* make her holiday. Please, please, I am—"

"*Mine,*" Jonas snapped. "Don't even think about it." He strode across the bullpen, more than aware that the other detectives had noticed her, too.

Christie wasn't wearing a Christmas sweater today. She was in all black—black turtleneck, black pants, and a long, sleek black coat. The woman looked so sexy he was suddenly hungry for a bite...of her.

She hurried forward. "Oh, good, I was hoping I'd catch you!"

He caught her. Jonas snagged her hand and tugged her toward him. He leaned in and kissed her, fast and hard. *Back off, Scotty.* And he figured all the other hungry jerks who were close by should get the message, too.

A wolf whistle split the air.

He expected Christie to break away at the sound, but, instead, her hands lifted and wrapped around his shoulders. She pulled him closer.

He let the kiss linger as he enjoyed her taste. *Enjoy?* Hell, he *loved* her taste. After a few moments, when he finally managed to pull back, her eyes seemed to shine even more.

"I was...um..." Her gaze darted around them. "This is the first time I've been in a police station."

He could believe it. Not like the Tates were hauled in a lot for questioning.

Her eyes narrowed, and she nodded. "I like the garland."

She would. If it was a Christmas decoration, she'd love it. And that was the moment he noticed her necklace. A thin gold chain circled her neck, a chain attached to a tiny Christmas tree.

A smile tugged at his lips. God, he absolutely loved—

No.

He dropped his hands and stepped back. "Um, Christie?"

Her eyes were still on the garland. Scotty had wound it all the way across the station.

Jonas's breath eased out as he stared at her. She was so beautiful. He could look at her for hours and never want to look anywhere else.

"Hey, man!" Scotty's hand slapped down on his shoulder. "Introduce me!"

Christie's gaze flew back at his partner's voice. She smiled a sweet, shy smile. One directed at Scotty.

Jonas growled, then cleared his throat and managed to say, "Scott McKenzie, this is Christie Tate."

"I'm his partner." Scotty offered his hand. A hand Christie foolishly took. The guy brought her hand up for a lip-smacking kiss. "You should call me Scotty. Everyone does."

She laughed, a quick but lush sound. "Nice to meet you."

She probably meant it, but only because she didn't know Scotty well yet.

Scotty frowned at her. "Tate...where do I know that name?"

"You've probably met my brother. Jonas and Daniel are old—"

Scotty snapped his fingers. "Tate Toys!"

She nodded. "Yes, I work—"

"My nephew loves the Ricky Rocket Shooter Robot!"

Christie beamed.

"The first time I saw that thing fly across the room..." Scotty shook his head and laughed. "I wanted one, too."

"I can get you one," she offered as a light pink stained her cheeks.

"Nah...those things sold out weeks ago."

"I've got connections." She bit her lip. "Actually, I made Ricky." The pink on her cheeks deepened at her rushed confession. "And right now, I'm working on Rover, his sidekick. It'll be a dog who can fly. He'll be remote controlled, too, and he'll interface with Ricky—"

"You're bullshitting me," Scotty said as he inched closer to Christie. "How the hell would you even go about making something like that?"

"Well, I studied engineering and robotics so—"

Jonas stepped in front of his partner before the guy could swallow Christie because Scotty was all but salivating over her. "Back off, *partner*. The lady and I need to talk."

Scotty's eyes squinted. "Lucky SOB." He stretched and peered at Christie over Jonas's shoulder. "Nice to meet you, ma'am. If you get bored with old Jonas here, you can—"

Jonas put his hand on Scotty's chest and shoved. "Why don't you get started on the Harris paperwork?"

With a smirk, Scotty sauntered away. "Fine. But I'll be back."

Jonas turned toward Christie. "Sorry about that."

She blinked. "About what?"

About the dick who was drooling over you.

He caught her hand and led her into the nearest empty interrogation room. At least they'd have some privacy there. He shut the door with a soft click. "About last night," he began. Oh, shit, there was no easy way to do this. Come to think of it, he'd never had to do this with his other lovers. "I'm sorry."

A little furrow appeared between her brows. "For what?"

"For jumping on you like I was starving." Or crazed. Or...*obsessed*. Which, fine, he was. Obsessed with her. Had been for years.

Her smile flashed again, and he saw her dimple wink. "But I liked what happened last night."

The thudding of his heartbeat filled his ears. They were alone. The door was closed. He could put her up on the table...

"I liked everything we've done." She lifted her hand and trailed her fingertips down his chest. "And everything we're going to do."

This was the shy Christie who'd barely looked his way over the years?

Then he noticed the pulse pounding too quickly at the base of her throat. He caught the slight tremble in her fingertips. From lust? Oh, sure, one very swollen part of his anatomy hoped so...

But her eyes had already fallen away from his, and she was easing away, a little too fast.

Fear? Was she afraid? Christie should know she had nothing to fear from him, and she didn't need to prove a single thing to him. Yet he had a lot to prove to her.

"You were right," he told her. His voice sounded gruff. "The case over the weekend got to me. Made me remember..." *Mom!* Her body. The blood. The scream that had burst from his throat. He sucked in a deep breath. "I wasn't in a good place when I came to you."

"I wanted you to come back to me." Her eyes met his and held. "I'm glad you did."

A man could only take so much. Carefully, gently, his fingers slid under her chin. He tilted her head back and let his lips whisper over hers. If those cops weren't out there, each one of them no doubt straining to hear what was being said, he'd devour her.

Tonight. The holidays weren't over. Not yet. He still had time with her. Time to make her want and need just as badly as he did.

"I'll come to your place after my shift tonight," he said against her lips. He loved that fireplace she had at her home. Loved the warmth behind him and her soft body beneath his.

Her hand pushed against his chest. "I...ah, that's why I'm here."

He couldn't help the tension that tightened his shoulders. *Is she calling things off already?*

"Actually…" She took a deep breath, one that made her breasts rise nicely. Distractingly. "I'm here because I was Christmas shopping in the area, and I realized I wanted to see you."

No lies. The tension slipped away from him.

"I could have called." She shrugged. "But I-I just came to see you. I hope that was okay."

Her uncertainty was plain to see, not hidden behind a too-bright smile, but obvious in the small, sexy stutter that had slipped free. He liked it when she showed her confidence, and, hell yes, he loved her vulnerability, too. When it came to her, was there a damn thing he didn't like?

Shit. *I'm in trouble.*

"I'm having dinner at my parents' tonight. A family Christmas get-together." Christie's words emerged in a rush. "You're welcome to come with me."

To the Tate house? He'd been there with Daniel before, but never for the big holiday party. He'd avoided the annual family party like it was the plague. To him, it was.

Christie's gaze searched his. "Not part of the agreement, is it?"

Just sex. Not family time. Not dates to celebrate.

"Forget it." She laughed. A laugh that sounded far too strained and fake for Christie. "It was just an idea. You don't have to come." She rose onto her toes and kissed his jaw. "We can meet tomorrow. We still have plenty of time."

But time could pass too quickly. Life could. "I'll be there."

Surprise flashed on her face. Delight. "You will?"

He managed a jerky nod. *What am I doing?* "We'll probably give your dad and brother a heart attack, but what the hell? Why not?"

This time, her laugh was real. "I think they'll both survive seeing us."

"I'll meet you there," he offered, thinking fast. "My shift ends at eight. I'll come by as soon as I'm done." *When I get there, I'll drink enough to make it through the glares Daniel will give me.* Glares and maybe a punch. Or two. Because he knew how his buddy would react.

"Then we can go back to my place." Her voice became huskier. "Or yours."

He thought about his place for two seconds. "Yours." He smiled. "I like the way your skin looks when the tree lights shine on you." On her breasts. On her sex when her legs spread for him. Oh, yeah, he liked that. Definitely.

A knock shook the door. "Captain wants us!" Scotty called out. His voice seemed way too happy for that announcement. No one was ever happy to talk to the captain.

Jonas pressed a quick kiss to Christie's lips. "I'll see you tonight." He opened the door and found Scotty standing too close.

Scotty grinned. "See you soon, Christie."

Christie murmured something nice and polite back to him. Jonas turned his head and caught sight of his desk, and the package still on top of it. He hurried forward and scooped it up. When he turned back around, Christie was already under the garland as she quickly headed for the exit. "Christie!"

She glanced back. Same welcoming smile. Same gorgeous eyes.

And the same punch hit him in the gut. Dammit. *What is happening to me?* He hurried forward and offered her the gift.

As soon as she saw the package, her skin flushed. "Jonas?"

"I was gonna give it to you tonight."

A detective's voice rang out, *"Ain't that sweet?"* The voice belonged to Bronte, a guy Jonas would pound later.

Her hands tightened around the box. "Thank you." She lifted the box to her ear and gave it a quick little shake.

God, she was cute. *Perfect.* Jonas kissed her. Fast but deep. "You can thank me after the party." She could do anything she wanted tonight.

He sure planned to do just that.
Anything. Everything. With her.

***

Christie waited until she was back in her car and then she ripped open the package. When the green silk panties tumbled out—thong underwear—she wasn't surprised.

She was turned on.

She knew just what she'd be wearing tonight for her detective.

Maybe she'd let him rip this pair off, too. It really depended on whether he was naughty or nice.

CHAPTER SEVEN

"So you're going to meet the family, huh?" Scotty asked as they grabbed their coats at eight and got ready to head out the door.

Another day from hell. Holidays could bring out the best in people, but they could bring out the worst, too. He and Scotty had spent hours at another crime scene. A robbery gone bad. The shop owner hadn't been the one to wind up in the body bag, though. The robber probably hadn't expected a guy in his eighties to fight back.

He had.

Jonas yanked on his gloves. "I already know the family." Too well, so he knew what kind of welcome he'd get when he showed up with Christie.

Because they also know me too well. Well enough to understand that he shouldn't be with

Christie. He wasn't good enough for her. He'd always known that truth, too.

"Take my advice with this one," Scotty said as his grin slid away. "Don't screw up."

Jonas raised a brow.

"Seriously. This one isn't like the others."

Christie wasn't like anyone else that Jonas had ever met.

"We're both gettin' too old to spend our holidays alone." Scotty looked out the front doors of the station. "There's got to be more than crime scenes waiting on us. If you're smart, you'll take that 'more' that's standing so close to you." He inclined his head. "Good night, partner."

A cold blast of air swept inside when Scotty left.

Jonas lifted his collar and got ready to follow his partner.

"Yo, Kirk!"

His hand hesitated in front of the doors. He glanced to the left and saw the desk sergeant waving him over. He and Carl Wallace had known each other for years.

"Hey, aren't you friends with Daniel Tate?"

A fast nod.

"My boy Jamie is working as a security guard there."

"I saw him the other night." *And he might have seen me and Chrnstie in the elevator.* Jonas turned away from the door. There was something in Carl's voice that had caused unease to slither through him. "There a problem?"

"I know it's not your beat, but, since you and Daniel are buddies..." Carl leaned over the desk.

"Jamie called about an hour ago. Said there was some trouble in one of the offices."

"What kind of trouble?" Jonas's phone vibrated in his pocket. "Hold on, Carl." He stepped to the side as he put the phone to his ear. "Kirk."

"Jonas! Shit, man, I need you." Daniel's voice was way more tense than normal—and normal usually *was* tense for Daniel. "Can you come down to the company? Someone broke into Christie's office and trashed the place!"

What? Fuck. "I'm on my way." He spun around.

"Wait!" Carl called out. "Don't you want to know—"

"On it, Carl, thanks." The cold air hit him in the face as he raced for his vehicle. *Christie's office.* What the hell? As far as he knew, there had never been any trouble at Tate Toys.

So why was it starting now? And why was some asshole targeting Christie?

***

Uniforms were on the scene when Jonas arrived at Tate Toys. A cop he recognized, Officer Larry Piner, stood just outside Christie's office doorway. Piner was questioning Daniel and jotting down fast notes.

Daniel caught sight of him. Relief flashed across his face. "Jonas! Thanks for coming so fast." Daniel ran a hand through his hair and gestured to Christie's office. "Can you believe this shit?"

Jonas inclined his head toward Piner, then let his gaze rake the interior of the office. Piner's partner was inside, carefully navigating through the wreckage. Papers and files littered the floor. The computer screen was busted into about a hundred pieces. The desk was overturned. The lamp smashed.

"You sure there was no one working here today?" Officer Piner wanted to know.

"I'm sure." Daniel's hand dropped. "Everyone on this floor is off the rest of the week for the holidays. Hell, everyone but the folks in distribution are off, and they're all down at the warehouse. We've only got a skeletal security staff in this building. No one else should be here."

"Any other damage?" Jonas asked, aware that a bite was in his words.

"Just Christie's office," Daniel replied.

Just Christie's office. Jonas didn't like that. Not one bit. Someone could be sending her a message. "What about cameras?" he asked as anger built in his gut. "You got them turned on, right?"

Daniel nodded his head in agreement. "We've got them downstairs at the entrance, but that's where a guard is posted. If anyone came in, he would have noticed."

Not if he'd been in the bathroom or on a break. "Get the tapes," Jonas ordered as he walked slowly into the office and surveyed the scene. "Have you called Christie?"

Silence.

He tossed a glance back over his shoulder. "You've called her, haven't you?"

"No." Daniel's lips pressed together. "It's so close to Christmas, and I mean, *look at this place*. I don't want her coming in here and seeing this crap!" His hair stood up, probably from Daniel running his fingers through it too many times. "Christie can't handle this stress right now, not on top of that whole mess with Charles. Hell, I just want you to find out who did this, and I want the jerk arrested!"

Jonas glanced toward the filing cabinet. Every folder had been yanked free, and the contents had been scattered across the floor. The drawers hung open, deep and empty. Jonas pulled out his phone.

"Are you calling in a crime scene team?" Daniel asked, and there was excitement in his voice. "Good plan. Let's *CSI* this asshole."

Jonas just shook his head and waited for the call to be answered. One ring. Two.

"Hello." Her voice was soft and husky.

He took a breath. "Christie, it's Jonas."

"What are you doing?" Daniel's desperate yell grated in his ears. "Did you just call my sister?"

Jonas ignored him. "I'm not going to be able to make that dinner tonight." No, he'd be working this case until he figured out what the hell was going on. "There's been a break-in."

"But..." He could hear her hesitation. Her confusion. "But you work homicide."

This case was different. *Personal.* "The break-in was at Tate Toys. It's your office, Christie."

"What?"

"I'm down here now with the investigating cops. I want you to come by. You'll know if anything is missing." He exhaled. *Stay calm. Don't freak out.* But he was freaking out. *Because this is Christie.* "If you'd rather, you can come in tomorrow and make a full list. You don't need to cut out on your parents—"

There was a rumble of voices in the background. Christie spoke to someone else, then she told him, "No, I'm on my way. Mom and Dad will hold dinner a bit. Don't worry, they've got plenty of guests here to keep things going."

"Be careful, baby." He ended the call and held the phone a moment as his gaze swept the wrecked office once more.

Someone tapped him on the shoulder. He turned around. Daniel glared at him. "You called her—"

"Christie had a right to know. She's not some fragile doll that's going to break with a little stress." He'd been wrong about her, and Daniel was, too. *All those years...she'd known.* Known his darkest secret, and it hadn't mattered to her. Hell, no, Christie wasn't going to break. She'd been right when she told him she didn't live in a castle.

Sure, she'd been sheltered. The Tate family had cosseted her in college. He'd helped by digging into old Benjamin's background. But Christie didn't need them to run interference for her. She was a grown woman. Strong, smart, sexy.

"*No.*" Daniel's eyes narrowed and his gaze seemed to shoot blue fire as he snarled, "*You called my sister 'baby.'*"

Shit.

"You're sleeping with Christie?" Daniel demanded.

A man's voice shouldn't get that strained and rough. Very bad sign.

Jonas got ready for the punch he knew was coming.

Daniel had a real killer right hook.

CHAPTER EIGHT

Christie hadn't dressed for the office. She'd dressed for him. Bought the new emerald green dress to match the panties. Maybe that was overkill, but she'd been feeling sexy at the time. Good thing she'd brought her coat with her. Otherwise she'd be flashing a lot of skin as she rushed down the hallway of Tate Toys.

Christie skidded to a halt on her two-inch heels—a very precarious halt—and she eyed the mess that was her office. *"Sonofabitch."*

Daniel was there at once, reaching for her. His tense face and eyes showed his worry. "It's okay, Christie, I know this is *upsetting—*"

"Yes, it's upsetting." Major understatement. "Some jerk ruined my office!" And her files. Oh, jeez, it would take forever to get those organized again. So many hours lost.

"Don't worry about this tonight." Daniel caught her hands and held them tight. "Just go back to our parents' place, relax, and—"

"Trust me, Daniel, I'm really not in the mood to relax." She was so mad her skin felt like it was burning. She craned her neck. "Where's Jonas?"

A muscle flexed in Daniel's jaw. "Jonas works the stiffs. You know he's homicide. We don't need him on a vandalism case. And it's just vandalism. I don't think anything was taken from your office."

Not taken. Just destroyed. "*I* need him."

"I was hoping you'd say that," Jonas announced from behind her.

Daniel swore.

She whirled around and found Jonas sauntering back from her lab area. As he came closer, she noticed the redness on his jaw. "Jonas?" She hurried back into the hallway so that she could meet him half-way and, luckily, she only nearly toppled once in her shoes. "What happened?"

"Must be something about your office," he told her as he came to a stop. His lips curled a little as he added, "It makes folks want to assault cops."

Her fingers skimmed his jaw. "What?" His words sank in, and her eyes widened. "Charles? Did he come back? Did he do this?" He'd actually hit Jonas? Had Charles been the one to trash her office, too?

"Nah, not him. Not this time."

"It was me." Daniel's arm brushed hers as he came to her side. "I punched the asshole." He glared at Jonas. "And he didn't punch back."

Jonas inclined his head. "Didn't arrest you either. Guess it's your lucky night."

Daniel rocked forward. "You're screwing my sister!"

No, he did not just say that. Christie slammed her hand on Daniel's chest. "No." She kept her voice quiet and cool. A real effort, but the new and improved Christie could manage that effort. "Your sister is screwing *him*." She didn't even stutter when she snapped out those words. Her head turned so she could see her brother's reaction.

Daniel's eyes bulged.

"And if you try to take a swing at him again..." Because that really pissed her off. She wasn't sixteen. She didn't need Daniel fighting her battles anymore. Fighting her battles or fighting her lovers. Hadn't she told him that enough times? "If you swing at Jonas again, I'll punch you." Her right hook was even better than his.

Daniel blinked. "Christie?" He sounded like he wasn't sure he was talking to his sister. His gaze had gone uncertain and his voice seemed hesitant.

She kept her hand on his chest.

"I told you she could handle a little stress." This came from Jonas.

More than a little. She'd been handling stress all her life. Try being thirteen in a room full of eighteen-year-olds—stress much?

Daniel's gaze bored into her. "Christie, you know what he's like."

She knew exactly what Jonas was like. She nodded. "Jonas is your best friend. He's had your back for years. He's strong and loyal and—"

"Not when it comes to women." Daniel lifted her hand from his chest and tried to tug her away from Jonas. She wasn't in the mood to be tugged. "When it comes to women, he's just like *me*."

She shook her head. "You're—"

"No commitment, Christie."

Jonas cursed.

"When's the last time I brought someone home for you to meet?" Daniel pushed. "Tell me when I introduced a date to you and our parents."

Never. He'd never brought anyone home for a family meet and greet.

"Sex is great. Sex is fucking fantastic." Daniel huffed out a breath. "But I'm not looking for forever right now."

Neither is Jonas. The words hung unspoken in the air.

She took a moment to make sure her voice wouldn't waver. A moment and a very deep breath. "I'm not a kid who needs looking after any longer."

"Christie—"

"I make my own decisions. I can pick my own partner."

"Damn right." Jonas sounded pleased, almost proud.

She ignored him. "I don't want forever."

Daniel's eyes slit so much he seemed to squint.

"Men aren't the only ones who just want— what did you call it?" She tapped her chin with the index finger of her left hand as she pretended to remember. "Ah, yes, fucking fantastic sex."

Daniel's jaw dropped.

She stopped tapping her chin. "Jonas and I understand each other. What's happening is between us. It doesn't concern you." Christie glanced at Jonas. His eyes were on her, and his expression—well, crap, what was wrong with him? He was glaring at her.

Glaring when she was trying to stop him from getting into another fight with her brother.

"Uh, Ms. Tate?" the uniformed officer called out tentatively.

Oh, no. No, no, no. She'd forgotten about the other cops. Their audience. Had they heard everything? How fast would this little conversation get repeated at the station? No wonder Jonas looked pissed.

She cleared her throat and peered over at the cop. He was standing near the doorway of her office.

"Since you're here, ma'am, we need you to do a sweep of your office and lab and determine if anything was taken."

"Right." She sucked in what should have been a cleansing breath. It wasn't. Christie stepped back and pointed at both Jonas and Daniel. "You two going to behave?"

Glares were her response.

"Fine." She shifted her focus to Jonas. "Feel free to arrest Daniel if he swings again, or if you want to punch back, we both know he's got a glass jaw." With that, she left them. With every step that she took, Christie was aware that her strong mask was about to shatter.

Her knees shook as she headed back toward her office. The damn heels twisted beneath her, and she almost went down hard. Only a quick grab of the wall saved her, the wall and—

Jonas's hand, catching her under her elbow.

"Sexy as hell, baby," he breathed the words in her ear and she realized her coat had come open to reveal the green dress. His gaze dipped to her breasts. "Sexy as hell," he whispered again, "but those shoes could be lethal."

He bent and ran his hand over her calf. A soft, sensual caress that had her breath catching.

He eased off her high heel. The left shoe, then the right.

Her feet touched the soft carpet.

"Watch your step," he told her, and for an instant, she couldn't move because the warning in his words was too heavy. Jonas wasn't just talking about walking. So about what? Them? The vandalism and destruction? She forced her shoulders to straighten as she pushed away from him. She grabbed the heels, clutching them too tightly, and even though she was tempted, Christie didn't look back as she entered her office.

***

"I don't know what kind of game Christie thinks she's playing." Daniel spoke only after Christie disappeared with Officer Piner. "But she's not up to handling you."

Jonas realized he was still staring after her. "Sometimes, I don't think you know her well at all." He slanted Daniel a measuring glance. Dangerous territory. He could well lose his friend over this situation.

She's worth it.

"You don't know her," Daniel snarled right back.

Actually, he did. "I know she's stronger than everyone gives her credit for." Stronger than he'd given her credit for in the beginning. Christie wouldn't break when reality shoved its ugly face before her. No, she wasn't going to break—period.

"So...what? You think that makes it okay for you to screw around with her?" Real fury vibrated in Daniel's voice. *"She's my sister! And you're not—"*

Jonas spun around. "Save it, Daniel." Daniel didn't need to say the words. *And you're not good enough for her.* Sure, he got that picture. Perfectly. "This isn't about you." Just her.

But Daniel blazed on as he snarled, "You're not the kind of guy who's going to settle down. Hell, until six months ago, you were a different man with every case you took! You loved that undercover life. Christie isn't like you—she *wants* stability. She wants a family. She wants forever."

But she'd only asked him for a few nights. She'd told him she *didn't* want forever.

Or maybe...*maybe she just doesn't want it with me.*

"I told her to be careful with you." Daniel crossed his arms over his chest. "I warned her, but she didn't listen."

"I'm not going to hurt her."

Daniel just glared back at him. Then he exhaled. "You've known her all these years. So long. Why now? Why'd you finally make a move now?"

Because you're right—until six months ago, I was a different man almost every damn day. I was drowning in the crime and the hate and realized I had to get out. And when I got out...there was Christie. As perfect and tempting as she'd always been and this time..."Because she wanted me."

"Plenty of women will have sex with you. You don't have to—"

"She *wanted* me," he said again. "She knew me, and she still wanted me." Dark shadows on his soul and all. "With Christie, I wasn't going to be dumb enough to turn away from her. Not even for the sake of our friendship. So just deal with it, asshole."

Daniel blinked at him. "Wait, wait. *Wait.* Man, are you saying—"

"I'm saying it's none of your business, and I'm saying the last thing you want to do..." Jonas let the steel ripple beneath his words because he was tired of explaining himself and tired of playing the nice guy. "The last thing you want to do is get between me and Christie." Because nothing would keep him from her, and the bond of friendship could only stretch so far.

Silence.

"I don't *think* anything is missing." Christie sounded uncertain as she appeared once more in the hallway, with the cops at her sides. "The files will take me hours to sort through, so I can't say for sure about them. But, I mean, I didn't have anything in my office that had massive value. The computer is still there—smashed—but there. The printer, all my photos—everything *seems* to still be inside."

Officer Piner—Larry—had his notebook out. "If something wasn't taken, then it seems like this was a personal attack against you."

Jonas forgot about Daniel and hurried to her side.

"Does anyone have a grudge against you, Ms. Tate?" Larry asked.

Her brows rose.

"Did you fight with anyone recently?" Larry's partner asked. He was a young guy with blond hair and ruddy cheeks.

Christie's gaze darted to Jonas. "There was an incident the other night. Right after the office Christmas party."

Daniel pushed closer. "What kind of incident?"

Her hand rose and caught the edge of her Christmas tree necklace. She pulled on the bottom of the tree and stretched the thin, gold chain. Her gaze returned to Larry. "A situation with my ex became a bit heated."

"What?" Daniel demanded. "Was Charles causing trouble? I knew I should have fired—"

"Does this Charles have a last name?" Larry interrupted.

"Charles Crenshaw." She dropped the necklace. It fell back into the lush cradle of her breasts. "But he wouldn't do this. He's an accountant, for goodness sake. He wouldn't—"

"Take a swing at a cop because he was jealous that you were with another man?" Jonas offered quietly. "I think you're underestimating the accountant."

Her lips thinned.

"I think so, too," Larry murmured. "And I think we're gonna be wanting to have a talk with Mr. Crenshaw." He inclined his head toward Daniel. "Is there any way he could have gained access to this building without being on the security camera downstairs?"

Before Christie had arrived, Larry had gone with Jonas to view the security footage. And they hadn't seen anyone. Only Jamie, the security guard. No one else had entered the building or left. Not until Daniel came by a little after seven.

Daniel frowned. "The cameras rotate. I guess if you knew the timing, you *might* be able to avoid them, but there's still Jamie. He would have noticed someone entering the building."

"But he didn't." Larry shut his notebook.

"Maybe we're looking at the time all wrong on this," Jonas said quietly. They'd only gone back over the current day's footage. "Maybe the attack didn't happen today. Maybe it happened after the party, and it was just discovered."

Maybe it happened when everyone was leaving. Too much activity. Too many people. The perfect time for an attack.

Sure, the computer would have made noise when it was smashed, but he'd seen for himself just how deserted this area of the building had been the other night. All of the action had been in the common areas. No one would've even heard the crash.

And there'd only been a few people left hanging around after Santa had finished all his deliveries.

He slanted a hard glance at Daniel. "Why'd you come to her office tonight?"

"I wanted to download some information on the projected development of Rover."

Right. Rover the Robot.

"I thought I'd show the info to Dad at dinner. Figured he'd get a kick out of it. He loves Christie's designs."

Jonas nodded. "So if you hadn't come by, no one would have even noticed the destruction until after Christmas." What a hell of a present for Christie to return and discover. Maybe that was what the perp wanted.

"I'll be needing Mr. Crenshaw's address," Larry noted.

"And I'll be coming with you to talk with the jerk." Jonas shook his head. "I knew I should have let that dumbass spend a night in jail."

Christie shook her head. "Look, Charles might have been angry, but he wouldn't do this. He backed off, remember? He knows things are over between us. Hell, he's already seeing someone else. Vicki Jasper. They'll probably get married one day and have little accounting babies." She shoved back a heavy lock of hair that had fallen over her cheek. "He's *not* the kind of guy who would destroy my office."

"Then who would?" Jonas asked, stepping close, catching her scent and wanting to touch her so badly that he ached. "Who else would do this? Who else would want to hurt you?"

If she'd give him a name, he'd get busy tearing the bastard apart.

Her stare held his. "No one. I can't think...*no one.*"

But someone was out there. Someone who had a grudge against her. Someone who was going to pay.

And Charles Crenshaw was at the top of Jonas's suspect list.

CHAPTER NINE

Jonas didn't go back to her parents' house with her. Her parents had saved dinner for her and Daniel. They'd even kept their guests waiting so they could all eat together.

Her father was furious about her office, and he kept tossing out threats left and right. Her mother seemed worried, but unlike Christie's father, she didn't rage. Her voice was quiet and concerned as she asked questions.

And Daniel—well, he still seemed pissed.

There was an extra seat at the table. An obviously empty seat. Christie had asked her mother to make room for Jonas, and Clara had. Room that wasn't needed.

"Christie, dear, what happened to your friend?" her mom finally asked in her soft, southern drawl just as they were beginning the second course. Maybe her mom was trying to take the focus off the vandalism. Maybe she was simply curious. Clara was known for her curiosity—ahem, nosiness—as much as for the slew of beauty pageant wins she'd racked up back in the day.

Christie's hold on her knife tightened. "Jonas is working on the investigation about the incident tonight." *Incident* sounded nice and vague. She really didn't want her aunts, uncles, and assorted cousins knowing that her office had been trashed. And that the person who'd done the trashing was quite possibly an ex-lover.

"Jonas?" A smile stretched across her mother's lips. "Oh, that's good to know. I'm sure he'll get to the bottom of this and—"

"No, Mom." A long sigh came from Daniel. "What Christie means is that Jonas can't be *here* because he's working the case."

"Such a shame," her mother said, still obviously missing the point. "I invite him every year, and he never—"

"Jonas was my date," Christie announced flatly.

"Your date?" Her mother blinked. Once. Twice. Then her smile widened and her blue eyes gleamed. "Oh, finally, you're picking an interesting man!"

Yes, she was. Her gaze shifted to her father. She knew he'd heard everything.

He lifted one eyebrow. "You know what you're doing?"

She nodded.

He picked up his fork. "I always rather liked Jonas."

What?

Her father aimed his fork at Daniel. "You like him, too, so don't be glaring at me, son."

"He's *dating* Christie. He is dating your daughter."

Her father glanced her way once more. "Then that makes him one lucky man."

Christie swallowed. "Thanks, Dad."

"I learned my lesson with you years ago, sweetheart." A grin edged across his mouth. "You weren't ever really interested in that Benjamin, were you?"

She shook her head.

"Sometimes love can make a man do crazy things." He dove into his plate, came back up, and said, "But my girl is wicked smart, and if she's chosen to be with Jonas, then that's fine by me."

Daniel hung his head. "He *is* a lucky bastard."

She thought about Jonas's past. No, he wasn't lucky. She was the one who'd had all the luck.

Daniel happened to look up at her in that moment. His eyes narrowed on her face. "Christie?"

People talked and ate around them. Her mother turned away to chat with a cousin. Daniel scooted toward Christie. "You...know, don't you?" he asked. His voice was low. Meant only for her ears.

She let her fork drop. "Know what?" Jonas's secrets were his. It wasn't her place to tell them.

"I'll be damned." Daniel's eyes swept her face. "He told you."

No, I already knew.

"As far as I know, he's never told anyone but me," he added.

Her temper began to boil. It had really been one hell of a night. The break-in. The fight between Jonas and Daniel. Finding out her ex might be gunning for her. "He told you because he trusts you, Daniel. You're friends, remember? Even if you are acting like a jerk, Jonas still sees you as his friend."

His gaze held hers. "I'm sorry," he said softly, slowly.

"Don't tell me," she muttered. "Tell *him*."

The doorbell rang. A long, echoing peal of sound, and Christie couldn't help it—her heart started to race.

Then a few moments later, Jonas walked into the room, and her heart nearly jumped out of her chest. His hair was swept back, and a dark coat stretched across his shoulders. He stopped when he saw the packed table. The spread of food. All those relatives.

Christie leapt to her feet and shoved back her chair. "Jonas!" She couldn't stop the wide smile that lifted her lips.

He smiled back at her. A hesitant curl of his mouth that made him look even sexier.

Daniel rose, too. "Come on over here," he called over the din of voices. "We've got you a seat waiting." Daniel's hand squeezed Christie's shoulder.

Jonas came around the table. His steps were a bit slow. The bulge of his weapon was gone. He'd been armed when he met her at Tate Toys. He'd been a cop then. Now, he was coming to dinner just as a man. *Her date.* Christie took his hand and pulled him down beside her.

Just sex? Who was she kidding? It had never been *just* anything with Jonas. With him, it was everything.

"Glad to see you, Jonas," her mother told him as she flashed her dimpled smile.

"Son, we've got plenty to eat," her dad said. He waved his hand over the table. "Help yourself."

Jonas blinked and shot her a questioning glance.

She squeezed his hand beneath the table. "It's Christmas, and you've been invited to our Christmas dinner for years." But finally, *finally,* he'd come to celebrate with them.

His fingers tightened around hers.

She had to swallow the lump that rose in her throat.

Daniel leaned toward Jonas and said bluntly, "Sorry for being a dick."

To which her mother immediately shouted, "Oh, Lord, language! Don't let Grandma Addie hear that kind of talk!"

"Too late!" Ninety-three-year-old Addie let out a pleased cackle because she absolutely loved that kind of talk.

When Daniel winced, Jonas laughed. His head tilted back, and a deep rumble of laughter shook his chest.

Christie stared at him, speechless, lost. So lost—in him.

Right then, she knew exactly what she wanted for the holidays. Not just sex. Not fleeting pleasure. *Him. Always.*

Too bad she couldn't have what she wanted.

***

Jonas followed her home. Kept her taillights in sight at all times. Kept her in his mind.

They hadn't been able to find her ex. Jonas had gone with the cops to Charles Crenshaw's house, but he hadn't been there. According to a neighbor, Charles had left town yesterday. An annual trip back to see his parents at Christmas.

So the guy *could* have trashed the office Friday night, then—calm as you please—driven to Cincinnati to visit his family.

But Jonas didn't like the whole situation, and until he got a better handle on just what the hell was happening, he planned to stay close to Christie. Not that staying close was any kind of hardship for him.

She pulled into her driveway and the garage door began to open. He followed her, aware that the routine seemed way too comfortable and easy. *Like I'm coming home.*

Bullshit, of course. Her place wasn't his home. Not even close. His home was the barren apartment over on Bentley. The place that hadn't even sported a Christmas tree until around noon. He'd picked the thing up during lunch. He'd been worried Christie would come to his place and, well, hell, the woman loved Christmas. He'd needed the tree for her.

He climbed out of his car and locked the vehicle. Christie waited for him by the doorway. A warm smile teased her lips. The same smile she'd given him when he'd arrived at her parents' place.

The smile that made him feel like he'd taken a punch in the gut.

For that sweet curve of her lips, he'd gladly take a hit any day of the week.

He hurried to her, aware of the grind of the garage door as it lurched back down. His gloved fingers slid down her cheek. Her dress was driving him crazy. He was pretty sure that had been her plan all along.

Christie laughed lightly and turned away. She unlocked the door and walked inside—

Then she froze. The lights in the den and kitchen blazed cheerfully, but Christie wasn't moving.

"Christie?" He reached for her.

"I turned that light off when I left." Her hand pointed to the kitchen.

Shit. He pushed her behind him. "Get in your car. Pull onto the street. Lock the car's doors and stay there." He took a step forward.

Christie grabbed his hand. "What are you doing?"

He had his phone out. "Calling for backup." And checking the place out. He threw her a hard stare. "Go, Christie. Now." He didn't want her around any danger.

Her delicate jaw tightened. "Be careful, Jonas."

"Always, baby."

She slipped outside, and he got ready to hunt.

CHAPTER TEN

Her house hadn't been trashed. As far as Christie had been able to tell in those brief moments before she fled, nothing had been taken. Just like nothing had been taken from her office. But Christie *knew* someone had been inside her place. She always turned the kitchen light off when she left. Always.

Someone had been inside and that person had turned it back on.

But she could tell by the way the uniforms on the scene were eyeing her that they didn't necessarily believe her story.

When Jonas came back to her side, she straightened away from her car. Christie hugged her coat tightly to her body as she asked, "Do you think it's Charles? Is he really trying to—"

"Charles is in Cincinnati."

A shiver slid over her. "Since when?"

"At least since nine a.m. I got a trooper who owes me a favor up there to check in on your ex. I didn't think you wanted me to mention it at the party with all those people there, but..." Jonas shook his head. "Crenshaw's not our guy."

So someone else wanted to scare her? Why?

"I want you to come home with me tonight." His voice was gruff. "Let the uniforms keep searching here."

"Do you think they'll find anything?" *Someone had broken into my house.* The goose bumps on her arms weren't just from the cold. Fear had lodged inside her.

His jaw hardened. "Doubt it."

"Someone *was* here, Jonas." She wasn't crazy. She *was* more than a little obsessive compulsive, and she always turned out that kitchen light when she left.

"I believe you. That's why I want you with me. Until I find out what's happening, I want to make absolutely certain you're safe."

She could be safe at her parents' house. At Daniel's. If she went with Jonas, she'd be getting a lot more than just safety. And that was exactly what she wanted. "Okay, but can I get some clothes first?"

His gaze raked her, hot in the cold air. "I'll take care of that for you."

She licked wind-dry lips. "What's happening, Jonas?" She didn't mean between them. The situation between them was way out of control. "Why is someone doing this to me?"

He opened the car door and ushered her inside. "I'm going to find out, baby. I promise."

"This isn't your case." No dead bodies—*thank God*—so no need for him to be investigating. "Daniel might have called you in before, but you don't have to keep working this."

"You're involved." His eyes glittered. "That means I'm involved, and I'm not backing off until I find out who is doing this to you."

Her hands tightened around the steering wheel. "I didn't mean for any of this to happen." Things had spiraled out of control. "It's all gotten so complicated." Even as she said the words, Christie caught the narrowing of Jonas's eyes.

"Baby, sex is complicated."

With him, it was. Complicated and hot and wild, and it was also exactly what she needed right then to banish the cold that snaked through her.

Someone broke in my house. Why?

"Keep the vehicle running and stay warm." He pointed to a cop standing near a patrol car and explained, "Harris over there will keep an eye on you until I get back."

She grabbed his hand. "You really think I need someone to watch me every minute?"

His stare bored into her. "*I* need him there." The faint lines around his eyes seemed deeper. "It takes someone real ballsy to walk right into your house. Whoever this dick is, he's not getting close to you again."

This wasn't the way her Christmas should have turned out. When she'd made her wish, she'd just wanted—

He kissed her. She expected a hard, fierce kiss. Instead, Jonas gave her the gentlest whisper of his lips against hers. "You don't need to worry.

Whoever this guy is, he won't hurt you. I'm the only one getting close to you."

Then he was gone.

And she wanted him back. Close again. As close as she could get him.

***

She'd never been to his apartment before. Christie wasn't sure what she'd expected, but the relaxed feel of the place suited Jonas. She liked the overstuffed couch—a couch that faced the giant TV. The overflowing bookshelf wasn't a surprise. She'd known Jonas loved to read.

But she hadn't expected the tree.

A small Christmas tree stood in the corner of his den. It wilted a little and sagged to the right. Some gold garland—like the garland she'd seen at the police station—had been tossed around the tree. No presents were under the tree. No tree skirt. No, um, water that she could tell. It wasn't an artificial tree, so it *really* needed some water.

Jonas came up behind her. "It's a piece of shit, isn't it?"

Despite the tension that had been riding her, Christie found herself laughing. "No, I think it's gorgeous." She'd always been a Charlie Brown tree fan. "But, Jonas..." She turned in his arms so that she could face him. "You might want to consider watering it. If you want the tree to live until Christmas, that is."

His cheeks stained a faint pink. "Figured I forgot something." He shook his head. "I knew if I didn't get a tree, you'd—"

Whoa. Wait a minute. "*When* did you get the tree?"

"Today." He bent his head and his lips pressed against her neck.

He was kissing her weak spot. She held onto his shoulders as her knees trembled. "Wh-why?"

He licked her neck. A slow, sensual lick. "Because you love Christmas."

Well, yes. She did. Didn't everyone?

He eased away from her. One step back. "There wasn't much for me to celebrate in the years after my parents died." His voice was hard. Rough.

No, there probably hadn't been.

"I bounced around in foster care until I hit eighteen. And then, hell, I met Daniel. Your brother invited me home every holiday, but I didn't go with him."

"Why not?"

"Because seeing other families hurt too much." He glanced toward the tree. Winced. "There were only a few trees left on the lot. I swear, it didn't look that bad earlier."

Seeing other families hurt too much. She swallowed the lump in her throat. "It just needs some water. The tree is gorgeous. Perfect."

But he shook his head. "It's not like yours."

"That's because I spent *two days* decorating mine, and I forced Daniel to help me." *Next year, you can help.* She held those words back. Barely.

There wouldn't be a next year. The wish she'd made had time limits. *We only have a little time left.* She closed the distance between them and wrapped her arms around his waist.

"When I worked undercover, I didn't have days off for the holidays." His voice seemed to rumble against her. "I didn't *want* my Christmas to be free."

But this year was different. He wasn't in Narcotics any longer. "Jonas, why'd you transfer out?"

Silence. Then, he finally replied, voice still too rough, "Because I realized there were things I *did* want. Things I wanted more than the job."

What do you want? The question trembled on her lips. The bolder, braver Christie would ask. But that woman wasn't there at the moment. Too much had happened tonight. Doubts surrounded her. Fears. "I hope you get everything you want," she said instead and meant it. Jonas deserved to be happy.

"So do I." He was staring down at her.

She couldn't read his expression. She wished that she could.

His mouth took hers. The kiss was hard. Deep. Hot. Body-meltingly-good and—

His head lifted as he growled, "I hope I get everything...because I'm damn well realizing how much I need you."

Wait—what had he just said? "Jonas—"

He was already kissing her again. His clever tongue thrust into her mouth. His hands pushed the coat off her shoulders, and it hit the floor.

The man knew how to kiss. How to drive her wild. When their mouths met, she ignited. Desire blasted through her body and she just wanted more and more.

"Did you wear this to drive me crazy?" Jonas demanded as his hands slid over the dress. His touch lingered around her hips.

It took a moment for his words to register. Then...She managed a nod. Yes, yes, her intent had been to make him crazy.

"It worked." He lifted her up, carried her, and put her down on the table near the wall. "I wanted you from the second I saw you tonight. You were nervous, scared, and I wanted to keep you safe—*and I just wanted you.*" His hand pushed under her skirt. "Oh, hell, *garters*? Are you seriously wearing garters right now?"

They'd been so sexy in the store, and she'd never worn them before. They'd looked great on the mannequin. Kinda naughty and fun. So she'd splurged for the hot garters and thigh highs.

"We're not making it to the bedroom, not for the first time." His blazing eyes held hers. "I'm fucking starving for you."

When had a man ever told her that? When had a man ever looked at her with such need?

No other man. Just Jonas.

"I don't need the bedroom." She let her hands trail down his chest. Thanks to the table, she was at the perfect height to touch and tease. And, really, it was her turn to play. She caught the buckle of his belt and unhooked the leather. He'd already ditched his jacket and gloves. Time for the rest to go.

He sucked in a sharp breath when she unsnapped his pants and eased down the zipper. "Wait."

Her exploring fingers stilled. He was telling her to stop? Her jaw almost dropped.

But he yanked a condom out of his wallet and slapped the foil packet on the table. Ah, yes, that was her man. Always prepared.

She reached for his cock. Already up, thick, and bobbing toward her. She hadn't gotten the chance to stroke him before. Hadn't been able to explore all of him because he'd been so busy touching and kissing all of her.

Now she had her chance. Christie squeezed his length, stroked his cock from base to tip and enjoyed the way he hissed out her name. He was warm, strong, and she knew he'd feel so good inside her.

She pumped him, over and over. Stroked carefully. Tightened her hold. Loved the way he tensed even more and—

He caught her wrist. Held her in a fierce grip. "Told you..." Need thickened his voice. *"Can't wait."*

Ah, but she was having so much fun. "You haven't seen my underwear yet." She kissed the hard line of his jaw even as her hand broke free of his grip so that she could continue working his cock. "Do you think I'm wearing your gift?"

She felt the shudder that worked through him. In the next breath, he shoved up her dress. The material hiked at her waist. Revealed the silk of her emerald panties.

His hands moved to her spread legs. Jonas's callused fingertips carefully slid under the garters. Rose up. Caressed her so tenderly. But the need that roared through her wasn't tender or soft. It felt savage. *"Jonas!"*

His finger edged under the panties. Found her core. He thrust two fingers into her. Withdrew. Thrust...

And stroked her clit.

Oh, God.

"Wet and tight." He grabbed the condom with his left hand, even as his right kept caressing her. His fingers slid in and out. "So fucking good."

She grabbed the packet from him. Ripped it open. She rolled it down his length and enjoyed the way his dick jerked toward her.

He positioned his cock against her. Christie's hands flew out and pressed behind her, slapping down against the wood as she fought to brace herself when he pushed deep, so deep inside.

Better than good.

Her breath panted out.

He started to thrust. Fast. Faster. The table shook beneath them. Trembled. No, was that her? The table? Oh, crap, they were going to break—

Jonas pulled her up against him and lifted her completely off the table. Christie wrapped her legs around him. She held on for the roughest and hottest ride of her life.

His mouth was on hers. His cock in her. She squirmed against Jonas, taking him even deeper. He held her fiercely with a steely grip at her waist. He took a few rough steps to the right, and her back rammed into the wall.

They didn't stop. Couldn't.

Deeper. Harder. Faster.

The pleasure hit her. It swept through her whole body as her sex clenched around him, and Jonas was right there with her. His cock jerked inside her as he came, and his mouth tore from hers. Their eyes met, held, and she watched the green of his gaze seem to go blind with pleasure. Pleasure that vibrated through her body. *So amazing. Nothing else has ever felt like this.*

When she could breathe, when the drumming of her heart wasn't the only sound she heard anymore, Christie realized she was still up against the wall. Still pinned by Jonas. He held her so tightly. Over his shoulder, she could see the tree. Slumping a little more now, but...*for me.* He'd bought that little tree for her. To make her happy.

She smiled and pressed a kiss to his shoulder.

Jonas eased back and stared down at her. Not glazed with lust and pleasure anymore, his eyes saw *her.* Maybe too much of her.

She tried to put on her confident front. "I don't think you ripped the panties that time."

One black brow rose. "Yeah, baby, I did."

Oh. She fought a smile. "Guess that means you owe me another present."

"Guess it means I do." His hands tightened around her hips. He stepped away from the wall, but still held her close. Jonas was so strong. Sometimes, she forgot just how powerful he was. *That strength is such a turn-on.* His muscles rippled beneath her touch as he carried her down the hallway. They turned and entered his bedroom.

She quickly took in the scene. Big bed. Dark blue comforter. Lots of room to stretch and play.

He lowered her onto the bed. Her fingers caught his jaw and felt the rasp of the stubble there. "Make me forget again," she whispered, knowing she was revealing a weakness, but with him, she didn't care. She trusted Jonas. "The only thing I want to think about tonight is you."

What would happen when the holiday ended? Would he go back to his cases? She'd go back to—what? Not another lover. Not after him. Who'd compare?

Not another accountant. Not another guy who fumbled around in the dark.

She only wanted Jonas.

I am so screwed.

"Baby, for tonight, I'm all yours," Jonas promised.

That was the problem. She didn't only want tonight. So how did she go about asking Santa for forever?

Especially when forever was against the rules.

CHAPTER ELEVEN

"I heard about the trouble your lady had at Tate Toys," Scotty said when he saw Jonas at the station the next day. "Hell of a time for something like this to happen."

It sure was. Jonas yanked out his chair. He didn't want to be in the precinct today. He wanted to be with Christie. She'd headed back to Tate Toys to sort through the mess in her office with Daniel. Before she'd left, Jonas had asked her if she was okay...

And that adorable chin of hers had jumped two inches into the air as she replied, *I can handle this.*

Sure she could, but he still wanted to be there with her. "Looks like someone was in her house last night, too."

"What?" A line furrowed Scotty's brow. "A vandal at work and a break-in at home? Man, that's not good."

"Tell me something I don't know." *That's why I should be with her.*

"Any leads?"

"Only one that was a dead end." But Charles Crenshaw *could* have been the one to trash her office. He'd been in the area the night of the holiday party. Hell, Crenshaw and the redhead had been the only two people he'd seen in that wing before he and Christie had left.

But even if Crenshaw had trashed her office on Friday, there was no way the man could have pulled that break-in at her house. Not unless the accountant was freaking Superman. *He can't be in two places at once.*

"She seems like a real classy lady, despite the fact that she's taken up with you." Scotty crossed his arms over his chest. "If you need any help on this, you let me know."

"Thanks, I will." He had to give a report to the captain, but after that, he was free and clear for the afternoon. He planned to spend that time focusing on Christie and the jerk who was screwing with her.

"I didn't realize she was the one to create Ricky Rocket Shooter." Scotty sounded impressed. "That thing's sold out at all the stores this year. Bet that next robot—what'd she call it— Rover? Bet he's gonna make a killing for Tate Toys, too."

Jonas paused. "Just how successful is Ricky?" There were no small kids in his world, so it wasn't like he spent a lot of time studying toy trends. He had no clue what the bestselling toys were for the holiday. Or...well, ever.

But Scotty knew his toys. His eyes lit up as he revealed, "I read an article the other day that said Ricky's number three on the list of the top ten toys for the year. *Number three.*"

Number three equaled a crap-load of profits for Tate Toys, and with Rover waiting in the wings...

Money. Greed. Always perfect motivators for crimes.

Maybe...

Maybe the perp searched Christie's office first. Looking for intel on the new toy design. When he didn't find what he was looking for, he went to her house.

And if the guy *still* hadn't discovered what he wanted? *He might go for the person who knows everything about the damn robot.*

Jonas grabbed his files. "Call Tate Toys. Make sure a security guard is on the floor with Daniel and Christie at all times." He'd tell the captain he had to go. The briefing could wait.

"All right, Jonas, sure, but wait—what are you thinking? You know who trashed her place?"

"I know that at this time of the year, people get desperate." He shook his head. "And money can make folks crazy." Folks you'd never suspect could cross the line if they thought the payoff was strong enough.

With Tate Toys, the payoff seemed to be *too* tempting.

***

Her house key was missing. Christie flipped through the keys on her key ring once more. She always kept backup keys in her filing cabinet. Last night, she'd checked through them quickly, and it had seemed like they were all there. No, *six* keys had been there. The right number of keys that should have been on the ring.

But two of the keys were wrong. Just extra keys that she'd never seen before. Substitute keys someone had placed on the ring.

Her house key and her lab key were missing.

Her gaze darted around the office. She'd spent an hour with Daniel as they worked on organizing all her files. No data seemed to be missing. Just her keys. Keys that had been carefully substituted so she wouldn't even realize they'd been taken.

"I know how he got into my house," she said, and Daniel's head whipped toward her. She held up the keys. "My backup is gone."

His eyes narrowed.

"And what else is gone?" Jonas asked as he appeared in the doorway.

Daniel and one of the day-time security guards, Sam, both turned to face him.

Her heart gave a little kick when she saw Jonas. That was normal, though. She always got a little boost when she saw him.

He filled the doorway, looking tall, strong, and dangerous. He had his badge clipped to his belt, and she could see the bulge of his weapon.

"I thought you were working at the station." Not that she wasn't glad to see him.

"I told the captain something important had come up." His gaze dropped to the key ring. "The lab key isn't on there, is it?"

Her fingers curled around the ring. "No."

Jonas waved his hand around her office. "This is all flash. A distraction. *You* aren't the target."

"Then why'd the jerk go to her place last night?" Daniel wanted to know.

"Because he's looking for something." Jonas glanced back down the hallway. "Something that would either be in the lab or in Christie's house."

Her breath rushed out.

"If I'm right," Jonas added, "this isn't personal, it's—"

"Business." Daniel jumped to his feet. "Someone's trying to steal our models!"

Jonas nodded grimly as his attention locked on Christie. "You been working on any designs at home?"

Her stomach knotted. "I took a prototype home for a few days."

"Let me guess." Jonas rolled his shoulders and the butt of the weapon peeked at her. "Rover?"

"Yes." The robot hadn't been working just right, and she'd wanted a chance to tinker with him over the holidays.

"Where's he now?"

"I brought him back last night. He was in my car and when you called about the break-in, I brought him back here." Her gaze darted to her brother. "And Daniel put him in the lab."

Jonas turned his gaze to Daniel. "Anyone else here today?"

"Ah, just Vicki from accounting. There was some kind of glitch with the payroll checks. She came in to—"

"All about the money," Jonas muttered. "I need to get in that lab, *now*."

Daniel shoved his hand into his jacket pocket. "I've got a key." He was already heading for the door. Nearly racing out with the silent security guard.

Christie was right on their heels.

They all rushed down the hallway. The faint melody of Christmas music filled the air as it drifted through the speakers.

"Let me go in first," Jonas ordered. "Then, Christie, I want you to do a sweep and see if all the Rover material is in there." He reached for the door, but didn't have to use the key. The lab was unlocked.

It shouldn't have been.

Well, hell.

He pushed open the door.

The Rover prototype was still there—and currently clutched in Vicki Jasper's hands.

"Vicki?" Daniel called out. Shock and anger mixed in his voice.

Vicki spun toward them. Her dark red hair swirled over her shoulders, and a wide, laughing smile spread over her face. "You caught me, Dan!" She gave a light, twinkling laugh as she put Rover back down. "I just had to sneak in and get a peek at old Rover." She dusted off her hands. "I was taking a break, stretching my legs a bit, and I—"

"How'd you get inside, Vicki?" Christie asked her, aware that Jonas and the security guard had both tensed at the sight of the other woman.

Vicki blinked her warm brown eyes. "The door was open. I walked in." A shrug. "Why? Is there a problem?" Another laugh eased past her lips, but this one sounded slightly nervous. "You left the door open. I just walked in to look around."

"We didn't leave the door open," Christie said with certainty. "We haven't been in here today."

"The room was locked tight last night," Jonas added, his voice cold and clipped. "I checked before I left."

Vicki's gaze flashed from Christie to Jonas. "Okay, um, I'm sorry I came in here." She began to edge away from the table. "Numbers can get a little boring sometimes. You know what I mean, Dan. You're a numbers guy, too. I wanted a little break." Her smile flashed again. "A chance to see how the other half lived."

Christie stared at her and felt sad. "You shouldn't be here, Vicki."

"No," Daniel said. His voice sounded heavy. Disappointed. "You shouldn't."

"What? You're going to fire me for walking in the playroom?" Vicki's eyes hardened. "Come on, what's this really about?" Now she was glaring at Christie. "Is it about me and Charles? Christie, look, we didn't mean for anything to happen, okay? We never meant to hurt you. We didn't plan it. We—"

"I don't care about you and Charles." But, wait, *when* had Vicki first hooked up with Charles?

Right after I announced plans for Rover at the company meeting. At least, that was the timeline according to office gossip.

"You're lying," Vicki snapped. "I know you're angry, but let's all calm down."

"We are calm, ma'am," Jonas assured her as he took a step toward Vicki. "Now I'm going to need you to do me a favor."

Vicki's gaze jumped to him. She must have seen the badge he wore because her eyes widened. Or maybe she'd spotted the butt of his weapon. Something caused alarm to flare in her gaze.

"I need you to empty your pockets. Real nice and real slow," Jonas directed her.

"What? I don't have to—"

"*Vicki.*" Daniel's voice snapped like a whip. "*What's in your pockets?*"

And she crumpled. Her lips trembled and teardrops slid down her cheeks even as she shoved her right hand into her pocket—and the hand came back up a moment later, holding two keys.

Christie was too far away to tell for certain, but her gut knew those were her keys. "Why?"

But it was Daniel who answered. "Because if there's one thing Vicki knows well, it's money. You ran the numbers for the project. You knew what we had coming, didn't you?"

Jonas took the keys from Vicki. She wasn't looking at any of them. Her head had sagged forward as she stared at the floor.

"She was probably planning to sell the prototype to a competitor." Daniel yanked a hand through his hair. "Vicki, this goes without saying but...*your ass—*"

"Is fired," Christie finished because even *her* Christmas goodwill had its limits. Vicki had passed those holiday limits. Actually, she'd blown right through them.

CHAPTER TWELVE

"Hot damn." Scotty held up his Ricky Rocket Shooter Robot, and a wide grin lit his face. "You get that you've just become the most popular guy at the station, don't you?"

Jonas let his brows climb. "I didn't do anything."

"No, but your girlfriend sent every cop in the precinct a Ricky Rocket Shooter Robot." He whistled. "If you make a cop's kid happy, you make a cop *very* happy."

"She and Daniel appreciate the PD's help." Help in nabbing Vicki before she'd walked out of the company with a prototype apparently worth more than a few years of Jonas's salary. "They wanted to do something to say thanks."

The captain came up and slapped Jonas on the back. "My son's been begging for this all year.

You know how hard it's been to find one of these little bastards?"

Not so hard for Christie and the folks in distribution at Tate. "If your son likes that," he said, "tell him Rover's coming next year."

"Thanks to you, he is." A soft, sweet voice. His favorite voice in the entire world.

Christie.

He spun around. She was there, just a few feet away. Wearing her long, loose cashmere coat and staring at him with a soft smile on her face.

He hurried toward her. The other cops milled around and shouted out "Thanks" and "Merry Christmas!" The gifts had sure put them all in good moods.

"What are you doing here?" Jonas took her hand and enjoyed the silken feel of her skin.

"I wanted to come by and make sure the robots were delivered safely." Her gaze swept the station. "If anyone was left out, let me know. Tate Toys can make sure everyone is covered." Her gaze returned to him. Warmed. *"Everyone."*

God, he could stare into her eyes forever.

"Jonas..." She nibbled on her lower lip. "Can we talk a moment?"

His heart rate kicked up. "Sure." He tugged her toward the back of the station. He couldn't use the interrogation room again. A suspect was inside. All the interrogation rooms were full. It was one of those days.

He tucked her into the far corner and braced his hand near her head, leaning in and effectively closing her off from the others. "Is something wrong?" Warmth was in her eyes, but she was biting her lower lip and her gaze kept darting away from him.

"You've helped me a lot in the last few days. You stood by me when the break-in happened at Tate. You gave me a place to stay—"

"Sweetheart, having you in my bed was no hardship."

She blushed, but carried on as she continued, "Then you handled Vicki and the fallout. I know you didn't need to be on the case and—"

He bent and pressed a quick kiss to her lips. "How many times do I have to tell you? You were involved, so that meant I was, too."

Her eyes searched his. What was she looking for? What did she want to see? If he didn't know, how could he give it to her?

"I broke the rules," she whispered.

He frowned down at her.

Her hand came up and pressed against his chest. "It wasn't supposed to happen."

Was that anger in her voice? Or fear? Either way, the woman had him worried. "What rules are you talking about?" Jonas wanted to know.

She swallowed. "Just sex. Not forever."

Ah. Yes. Those rules.

"I asked you not to lie to me, but I came here because I need to tell you...I'm the one who's been lying." She released a long breath.

What?

"From the beginning, I-I've been lying, Jonas."

The din around him seemed too loud. Too many phones were ringing. Too many voices buzzing. Scotty had started a round of "Jingle

Bells," and too many tone-deaf cops had joined in for the song. "Run that by me again."

Her body trembled against his. "I've been lying to you from the beginning."

She looked so beautiful that it hurt him to stare at her, and the twist in his gut told him he shouldn't ask but, "What did you lie about?" *Wanting me?* No, hell, *no*. The lust between them had been real. The pleasure too good to be faked.

"I want more."

He shook his head. Dammit, he couldn't hear her. He took her hand and looked for an option to—*ah, ha. There*. He shoved open the precinct's back door, and they rushed outside. The lightest flakes of snow had started to fall. "Tell me again," he said. The fury and fear in his blood were too hot for him to feel the cold. "Tell me what you want." Was she cutting him loose now? Right before Christmas?

It was the last thing he'd expected. He thought of the present he'd bought for her earlier. Tucked nice and safe in his desk drawer. Hell, no, this couldn't be happening. "My time's not up yet." Shit. He sounded desperate. Because he was.

"I know." She tugged her hands from him.

"What do you want, Christie?" *I will give you everything. Just give me the chance.*

"I want you." The snowflakes caught in her hair. She drove her hands into the pockets of her coat and rocked back. "I didn't just want a good time that first night. Didn't just want any man at the Christmas party. I wanted *you*. It's always been you."

He stared at her.

"I've wanted you for years." Her lips lifted in a smile, but her dimple didn't flash. "Guess that night at the party, I finally got brave enough to go after what I wanted." Her shoulders slumped. "But deep down, I'm *not* brave. I'm scared, I'm nervous, and right n-now, staring at you..." Her laugh was weak. "I feel like I'm making the worst mistake of my life. I probably should keep my mouth shut and enjoy the time we have left, but— *I made the wrong wish.*"

His heart was about to burst right out of his chest. "What wish did you want to make?"

She looked up at the sky. At the falling snowflakes. They kissed her lashes and whispered over her cheeks. "I don't want you just for the holidays."

His hands curled into fists.

"I've watched you over the years, Jonas. I've seen the women come and go, and I *know* you're not looking for some commitment."

Why the hell did everyone keep saying that? *Because that's the way I used to be.* Not anymore. Not with her.

"But that's the kind of woman *I* am. I might have pretended I wasn't—I might have said I just wanted the pleasure, too, but with you, *I want more.*" Her gaze came back to him. Met his stare directly. "I'm not going to lie anymore. Not to you. Not to myself. *I want more.*"

"More?"

"Not just sex. Don't get me wrong." Her words tumbled out. "The sex between us is incredible."

A uniform stumbled past, eyes wide. Jonas growled at him.

The young cop scurried away.

Christie lowered her voice as she revealed, "I like staying in bed with you. I like being there for you when you come back from a hard case. I like knowing that you'll be there for me when I need you."

I will always be there, sweetheart.

"I like it when you're with me and my family." Her breath blew out on a white cloud. "Jonas, I just like it when you're with me."

The cold still hadn't touched him. Couldn't, not the way his blood pumped so fast and hot. "Christie..."

She straightened her shoulders. "I had to tell you how I felt. I'm going to start doing that, you know. Telling people what I really feel and think. Life's too short to waste, isn't it? If you don't take chances, then you can't—"

He pressed his lips against hers and tasted the snow and the strawberries that he'd always crave. "When you're nervous," he whispered, "you talk fast. Did you know that?"

Her eyes widened.

"You don't need to be nervous around me. Haven't you realized that yet?" He eased back.

"No, you're wrong. You're the one who makes me the most nervous." Her gaze never wavered as she told him, softly, "Because you matter to me."

His heart jerked hard in his chest. "Not just sex, huh?"

Her head shook. "It never was. Not for me. I shouldn't have let you think—"

"It wasn't for me, either, baby."

And just like that, Jonas found out how to make Christie Tate speechless. She stared at him a few seconds with her mouth hanging open. "Wh-what?"

Her faint stutter squeezed his heart.

"The first time I saw you, you were wearing a pair of glasses with black rims. You had on jeans that were two big, sexy black boots, and a blue shirt that made your eyes even darker."

"Th-that was years ago. I don't even...how do you remember that?"

"Because, baby, I remember everything about you." Always had. "I knew the minute I saw you that you were too good for me." His smile flashed. A real smile. One he didn't have to fake. With her, he never faked. He just...was. "You were too young for me. Too young and too good, and I tried to stay the hell away from you."

The snow fell harder.

"I knew I was going into undercover work. I knew what it would do to me." He still didn't want her to know the places he'd been. The things he'd seen and done. Christie—she was the light he'd held close all those years, and she didn't even realize it. "But I had to take those jobs." Would she understand the driving need that had haunted him for so long?

Blood. Death.

"I know you did," she said, her voice a bit sad. "But Jonas, you didn't have to do all of that alone."

His hands rose to curl around her delicate shoulders. The woman would break him one day, if he wasn't careful. But with her, he'd always tried so hard to be careful. "Do you know why I left Narcotics?"

She shook her head, and the snowflakes drifted through her dark hair.

"I wanted something more." If he was going to tell her, he'd do it right. *Go all the way.* "No, screw that. I wanted someone. I wanted you."

"Jonas—"

"You never dated anyone seriously. I thought—fuck, I don't know what I thought." *That you felt the connection, too. That we would be together one day. That there was plenty of time.* Then he'd seen her with another man one day when he'd gone to Tate Toys to meet Daniel for lunch, and Jonas had realized time had run out. If he didn't act, he'd lose her. "Do you know why I was playing that Santa gig? When I'd barely celebrated Christmas before?"

"I thought you were a replacement—"

"Because you were going to be there. You weren't the only one who wanted something special for Christmas this year. I did, too. I wanted you. I wasn't going to sit on the sidelines any longer. Wasn't going to let life pass me by while I—" *Tried to slay demons who were long dead.* "While I just watched you go."

She blinked, once, twice, and then her dimple flashed. "Jonas, did you know?"

"Know what?"

"When you're nervous, you talk fast." She rose onto her toes and looped her arms around his neck. "I'm not going anywhere."

He pulled her closer. As close as he could get her. "Neither am I."

Her lips trembled, but not because of sadness. They trembled and stretched into the slow, sexy smile that had stolen his heart years ago. "New rules?" Christie asked.

"Damn straight."

"Sex."

"Lots of it."

"The *best* sex."

"With you, that's what I always have." Not just sex, so much more. He'd known that from the first touch.

"Strings?" she asked softly.

"Enough to tie you up." *Forever.*

She laughed, and he kissed her the way he needed to kiss her. Long and deep and hard. He'd finally gotten just what he wanted for Christmas. Christie—in his arms.

Just what he wanted—and everything he needed.

***

Christmas Eve. This year, Jonas wasn't spending it undercover with a bunch of asshole criminals he hated. He wasn't at the station, manning the phones.

He was in bed with Christie. His body relaxed. Sated from the sex. *The best.* Hell, yeah, sex with Christie—making love with Christie—was the best, and he'd be ready for another round soon. They had too many years to make up for, and he was too hungry to hold back.

His hand slowly trailed up the smooth curve of Christie's back. She stretched into his touch, then turned her head toward him.

Jonas leaned forward to kiss her. "One more rule," he told her, whispering the words against her mouth.

Her brows came together. "What do you mean?"

"Come with me. I'll show you." He slid from the bed and quickly pulled on a loose pair of sweatpants. Christie followed. She paused only long enough to snag the silk robe he'd bought for her. It was a blue to match her eyes.

When they went into his den, the little tree was glowing. Christie's touch. They'd decorated it together last night. Decorated. Drank wine. Laughed. Made love while the snow fell.

Presents were under the tree. Some for her family. Some that Christie had brought over for *him*. Even one for Scotty.

And a special one for her.

He pulled her down in front of the tree. Jonas reached for the small red box with the bright green bow.

Christie laughed. "Ah, I see. You want to start a tradition, huh?"

He turned back and caught the sexy gleam in her eyes.

"I'm all for that," she murmured with a wink. "And by last count, you *do* owe me another pair."

She took the box from him, and, as was her way, she lifted it up to her ear. Her grin kicked up as she shook the box.

Then her smile faded. "Wait. That doesn't sound like—"

"Open it," he urged her. His voice was rougher than he'd intended, but Jonas knew that this moment might just be the most important one of his life.

She stared at the box, then ripped the bow off and tore into the package.

When she opened the ring box, he held his breath. His heart didn't even seem to beat.

"Jonas?" She looked up at him. Her eyes were so wide and gorgeous.

"I don't want to have any more Christmases without you." He lifted the ring from the box and offered it to her. His fingers were shaking. "I told you there was one more rule. This time, I want forever." *Please, baby. Give me forever.*

She looked at the ring. Then at him.

"Please, Christie." His voice was so rough. "Will you marry me?"

She lifted her hand. Wiggled her fingers. "If forever is what you want, then that's exactly what you're getting."

"Is...is that a yes?"

"It's a hell yes."

Hell, yes! He slid the ring onto her finger. It was a perfect fit.

"You've been very good this year." She leaned toward him and brushed her lips over his.

Not good enough for her. But he'd try to be. For the rest of his life, he'd try to make everything good enough for her.

She pulled back and stared into his eyes. "I love you, Jonas Kirk."

"And I love you, Christie Tate."

"Merry Christmas."

He kissed her. He loved her mouth. Loved *her*. His arms curled around her. *Christie*. The woman he'd watched for so long. The woman he'd needed. The woman who'd given him a *really* good time that he'd never forget during the holiday season.

The woman who'd just promised him forever.

Now, Jonas had everything he wanted, right there, in his arms.

His only Christmas wish? It had been...her. To have a chance with her.

But they didn't just have a chance. They had a whole happily ever after.

"I think we both made the good list," he told her.

Christie nipped his lower lip. "I believe we could score some points on the naughty list, too." She pushed him down beside the tree. Lights gleamed around them.

"Baby, I am all for being naughty."

She straddled his hips. Smiled down at him.

He caught her hand. Brought it to his lips. Pressed a kiss to her knuckles as the ring sparkled in the light. "Merry Christmas, baby."

Merry Christmas.

THE END

A NOTE FROM THE AUTHOR

Thank you for reading DECK THE HALLS. I absolutely love the holiday season! Everyone seems happier, and, for a little while, the world is filled with magic. I always count down the days to Christmas with eager excitement, and I love to pass those days watching holiday romances on TV...and snuggling up to read holiday romances with a nice glass of wine! I hope this story puts you in a fun, holiday mood!

If you'd like to stay updated on my releases and sales, please join my newsletter list.

https://cynthiaeden.com/newsletter/

Again, thank you for reading DECK THE HALLS.

Best,
Cynthia Eden
cynthiaeden.com

ABOUT THE AUTHOR

Cynthia Eden is a *New York Times, USA Today, Digital Book World*, and *IndieReader* best-seller.

Cynthia writes sexy tales of contemporary romance, romantic suspense, and paranormal romance. Since she began writing full-time in 2005, Cynthia has written over one hundred novels and novellas.

Cynthia lives along the Alabama Gulf Coast. She loves romance novels, horror movies, and chocolate.

For More Information

- *cynthiaeden.com*
- *facebook.com/cynthiaedenfanpage*

HER OTHER WORKS

Wilde Ways

- Protecting Piper (Book 1)
- Guarding Gwen (Book 2)
- Before Ben (Book 3)
- The Heart You Break (Book 4)
- Fighting For Her (Book 5)
- Ghost Of A Chance (Book 6)
- Crossing The Line (Book 7)
- Counting On Cole (Book 8)
- Chase After Me (Book 9)
- Say I Do (Book 10)

Dark Sins

- Don't Trust A Killer (Book 1)
- Don't Love A Liar (Book 2)

Lazarus Rising

- Never Let Go (Book One)
- Keep Me Close (Book Two)
- Stay With Me (Book Three)
- Run To Me (Book Four)
- Lie Close To Me (Book Five)
- Hold On Tight (Book Six)
- Lazarus Rising Volume One (Books 1 to 3)

- Lazarus Rising Volume Two (Books 4 to 6)

Dark Obsession Series

- Watch Me (Book 1)
- Want Me (Book 2)
- Need Me (Book 3)
- Beware Of Me (Book 4)
- Only For Me (Books 1 to 4)

Mine Series

- Mine To Take (Book 1)
- Mine To Keep (Book 2)
- Mine To Hold (Book 3)
- Mine To Crave (Book 4)
- Mine To Have (Book 5)
- Mine To Protect (Book 6)
- Mine Box Set Volume 1 (Books 1-3)
- Mine Box Set Volume 2 (Books 4-6)

Bad Things

- The Devil In Disguise (Book 1)
- On The Prowl (Book 2)
- Undead Or Alive (Book 3)
- Broken Angel (Book 4)
- Heart Of Stone (Book 5)
- Tempted By Fate (Book 6)
- Wicked And Wild (Book 7)
- Saint Or Sinner (Book 8)
- Bad Things Volume One (Books 1 to 3)
- Bad Things Volume Two (Books 4 to 6)
- Bad Things Deluxe Box Set (Books 1 to 6)

Bite Series

- Forbidden Bite (Bite Book 1)
- Mating Bite (Bite Book 2)

Blood and Moonlight Series

- Bite The Dust (Book 1)
- Better Off Undead (Book 2)
- Bitter Blood (Book 3)
- Blood and Moonlight (The Complete Series)

Purgatory Series

- The Wolf Within (Book 1)
- Marked By The Vampire (Book 2)
- Charming The Beast (Book 3)
- Deal with the Devil (Book 4)
- The Beasts Inside (Books 1 to 4)

Bound Series

- Bound By Blood (Book 1)
- Bound In Darkness (Book 2)
- Bound In Sin (Book 3)
- Bound By The Night (Book 4)
- Bound in Death (Book 5)
- Forever Bound (Books 1 to 4)

Stand-Alone

- Never Gonna Happen
- One Hot Holiday
- Secret Admirer
- First Taste of Darkness
- Sinful Secrets
- Until Death
- Christmas With A Spy